sea
of
ruin

ALSO BY ANTON BRINZA

The Coyotes' Cross Prowler *(released 2026)*

The Entire Goat (Entrails Included)

Strike, Stay Your Hand

Sea of Ruin

Short Stories

Anton Brinza

For Stephanie
Don't be scared, little sister

Contents

Sea of Ruin   1

Get to the Root of the Problem   43

Bearded Vulture   61

In Case of Emergency   116

The Hogs of Aie Valley   143

Acknowledgments   185

About the Author   187

SEA OF RUIN

I

THE SURF WASHED AGAINST THE STONES, FILLING THE NIGHT air with a haunting white noise. Instead of the softer push and pull on sand, the hollows between stones created an echo effect, like distant thunder each time the water receded. Sometimes, the stones shifted, clattering and clunking as though someone were walking along the waterfront when no one was there.

"Want a beer?" Josh reached into the tote bag. The image of the owl on the bag gazed at him dumbly.

Whoooo...are you looking at?

"Lil?"

Lily didn't respond. She was staring distractedly toward the long, concrete pier at the southern end of the beach. Tall lampposts cast a mellow orange gleam over the fishing boats moored alongside it.

"Hey, Lil? Now or later?"

"Huh?"

"A beer?"

"They're in the tote bag..."

"I know, I—" When he cracked the first can, Lily jumped. "Hey. You alright?"

"What? Yeah, fine. It's just... Do you see that?"

"What?"

"That guy standing there."

Without raising her hand, she lifted a finger to point. Josh leaned over, searching between the boats. About halfway along the pier stood the hulking silhouette of a man, black beneath the curdled lamplight.

"Must be the last fisherman," he said.

"But why is he just standing there?"

Josh shrugged and slurped from the beer can. "Probably having a smoke or something. Doesn't feel like going home to his nagging wife just yet?"

"It's creepy. It looks like he's watching us."

"Don't be silly. You can't tell that from here. And if he is, he's probably thanking us, the tourists who keep this podunk village alive. Hey. Don't worry about it. Here." Josh shoved the beer into his wife's hand.

"Yeah. Yeah, you're right." She chuckled, sighed, then turned to face him, taking a long drink from the can. Josh popped a second can and clinked it against hers before chug-ging half of it. They shared a look, one of those peculiar looks that couples sometimes share, where it feels almost like you're living in the same skin.

They had both been to stone beaches before, but Mangchi Mongdol Beach was different. Most of the stones were the size of softballs, though plenty were as big as cantaloupes. Half a dozen picnic tables with parasols lined the rocks at the center of the beach. Clouds hung lazily about the sky, but there were still more stars visible than back home in Seoul, even on a clear night.

The beach stretched a fair way along the bay's western shore. A nice photo spot in the daytime, but that was about it. Across the bay lay Gujora Beach, with fine sand and a gentle grade. By noon the next day, Gujora would be overrun with couples and families while Mangchi Mongdol would remain relatively unpeopled, much like it was at this late hour.

Of the few groups that had spent the evening here, only a rowdy bunch of college students remained. They sat at another picnic table with a full spread of junk food, flirting obnoxiously, and incapable of putting down their phones. When they finished their cup noodles and beer, they walked up the steps to their pension, leaving their trash for the gulls to scavenge.

Finally, Josh and Lily had some peace and quiet.

"I can't believe it's been a year already," Lily mused.

"Me neither." Josh took another sip and gazed out to sea. Moonlight danced atop the gentle waves. "And to think they said we'd never make it."

"What?" Beer spurted from Lily's mouth and dribbled down her chin. "*Who* said that?"

"Uh..." Josh giggled, averted his eyes, kicked the rocks at his feet. "My mom."

"No shit. She announced it to everybody at the wedding." A double gulp from the tallboy helped to wash down that memory. "Who the hell else?"

"Nobody." Josh kicked the rocks again. He bent down to examine one. "Just Ronnie and Jane."

This time, Lily spat out an entire mouthful. Beer sprayed all over the picnic table and tote bag. Droplets dabbled Josh's cheeks.

"Ron and Jane don't think we're good for each other?" Lily croaked, still clearing beer from her throat.

"They do! *Now* they do. But they didn't. When we were dating, they, uh... Never mind. Forget it."

"*What?!*"

"They'd kill me if I—"

"Tell me, Josh, or I'll hold out on you for the rest of the summer."

Tittering mischievously, Josh raised his hands in concession. "Okay, okay. They used to place bets. They arranged a kind of pot with some of our other friends. You know, like which one of us would break it off first, who would cheat on the other, what the blowout fight would be about. And then, before the wedding, Janie was sure you would bail."

"That bitch," Lily laughed. "Wait. So you knew about this?"

"No! Ron told me at the bachelor's party. How do you think they paid for our tickets to Bali?"

The surf crashed against the stones. Lily stared blankly at Josh, her thoughts wrangled by memories. The perfect week they'd spent in Indonesia for their honeymoon now seemed tainted somehow.

"We won their pool, Lil." Josh gave a wicked grin. "None of their stupid predictions came true, so they couldn't pay out the money they'd collected. They didn't feel right keeping it, and Ron wasn't supposed to tell me about it. But, you know...

that night got pretty wild. You know how he is when he drinks. You'd never believe what else he told me—"

"Those tickets cost over three grand! That many people bet *against* us?! Those duplicitous fucks. They're supposed to be our friends!"

"Calm down, Lil. We beat their stupid pool. *We won.*"

Though Lily looked furious, Josh could not hold in his laughter. To avoid making her more upset, he stood up with his beer and began to shimmy, his hands held up, bobbing from side to side in the same dumb dance they always did to lift each other's spirits. Seeing him do it out here in this strange environment, away from home, away from the day-to-day, she couldn't help but crack a smile.

"Besides," added Josh as he gave her a peck on the cheek, "they were happy to give us such a nice wedding gift."

"But they didn't even pay for it."

"They did. The pool only had fifteen hundred or so. They paid the rest out of their own pockets."

"*Pshh.*" Lily gazed up at the corner window of their pension, where their friends were sleeping. "Serves them right. Assholes."

Laughing raucously, Josh sat down across from her. The picnic table creaked under his weight.

Geoje Island, the second largest of South Korea's thousands of islands, had won the lottery for the yearly getaway with their friends, Ron and Jane Cauldwell. This was their first trip together since Josh and Lily's wedding last summer, and also the first time Ron and Jane brought their two children along. It had always been just the four adults, the kids remaining back in Seoul with their nanny. With the kids in tow, the essence of the annual trip necessarily became more family-friendly. In years past, the four of them would have stayed up drinking at this picnic table until dawn, after which they'd pass out in their shared pension for a few hours and then move to the beach to resume drinking.

Gina and Helix were good kids. Six and four years old. Cute as hell. Well-behaved, if not a bit spoiled. But having them around sure changed the dynamic.

"Why don't we fire up these cigars?" suggested Josh, reaching into the owl tote again. "Won't be able to tomorrow with the kids around."

"Josh."

"Yeah?" He was digging around in the tote bag for the cigar cutter.

"He's still there. I think, um... I think he's coming closer."

Josh found the cutter and looked up. Lily was right. The man had moved down the pier toward the shore. At the moment, he was standing still. With the shadows, it was impossible to tell which direction he was facing, but it definitely felt like he was looking at them.

"He's probably just, you know..." Josh trailed off.

"Just what?"

"I don't know. Taking a leak or something. Staring at the water and contemplating life's deep quandaries. Hey." He reached out and grabbed his wife's hand, tugging gently to turn her attention away from the mysterious figure. "It's alright. Nothing's going to happen." He glanced over his shoulder at the stone shore, hoping to find a few other late-night beachgoers. The waterfront was empty. Had been since that noisy group left. But the pensions along the road were full with summer travelers, so it wasn't as though no one was around.

"I don't like this, Josh. We should go in."

"Lil, hey. I won't let anything happen. Do you want me to go and see what he's doing?"

"No, just... No. Let's light the cigars. But keep an eye on him, okay?"

They snipped the ends off their cigars. Lily laughed at Josh's poor cutting job, which left the wrapper flayed and flaky. She flicked the lighter, allowing the flame to lick her cigar. Josh watched the hypnotic, curling flames, then stood and walked toward the water. Walking on the rocks was not easy. They were smooth and rounded by years of salt water washing over them. They might shift underneath you at any moment. Twisted ankles had to be a serious hazard around here, especially for people wearing flip-flops. While Lily managed to walk on them barefoot without much trouble, Josh found it nearly impossible.

At the water's edge, the stones were slippery. Josh carefully squatted down, picked up a long, flat rock the size of a dinner plate, and underhanded it into the ocean like a bowling ball.

"Nice throw, Hercules," Lily laughed. "Made it all of two meters."

"Laugh it up, lady," Josh answered, trudging back up the stones. "Next, we'll see how far I can throw you. You done yet?"

As Josh sat down, Lily puffed on her cigar. She exhaled a thick plume. He looked up and, through the smoky sheen, saw the lone dark figure on the pier.

"Huh," he grunted as he started torching his cigar.

"What?"

"Nothing."

"Josh..."

"No. It's just...he moved again. He's standing at the top of the stairs leading down to the beach."

"Oh, shit. Josh. Let's go."

They were both openly staring at the man now. Josh sucked on his cigar, pulling the flame into the tobacco and squinting through a steady stream of smoke.

"No..." he said after a moment. "We sound ridiculous. He's just some old villager. Probably has arthritis all over his body and can barely walk from hauling fishing nets all day long. Just wait and see. He'll walk off the pier any second now, right up the road and into the village."

"And if he comes down onto the beach?" Smoke curled from Lily's lips as she spoke.

Josh shrugged. "It's a public beach, Lil."

For a few minutes, they puffed on their cigars, trying not to dwell on this other inhabitant of the lonely beachfront. The musky aroma of the smoke soothed and distracted them.

Five years ago, they met for their second date at an upscale cigar lounge in the Hannam neighborhood of Itae-won. Smoking cigars had remained one of their favorite ways to pass an evening together. They both described it the same way—it was like having a conversation without words. They would stare at each other, transfixed by the plumes of smoke pouring out of their mouths, the blue-gray sheen hovering just overhead, the red coals glowing when they pulled on them. They spoke in spurts while smoking, though there had been times when they burned entire Cohibas without sharing a single word. These were not uncomfortable silences, but the sort that drew them closer together. Years after that fateful second date, Josh and Lily both independently came to the conclusion that that was the night they fell for each other.

Wrapped in their smoky bliss on Mangchi Mongdol Beach, celebrating their first complete year as a married couple, they both began to relax. How could they not? The lapping of the surf on the rocks, the moonlight skittering over the rolling waves, the utter silence of a small Korean fishing village. They were still full from their dinner with Ron, Jane, and the kids. They'd ordered enough grilled sea eel to feed a party of ten. Their minds drifted. They thought about the future they were planning. Moving back to the US so Lily could get her Green Card. Starting a business together. Having kids of their own. Yearly trips back to visit Lily's folks in Seoul. That was all a few years off yet, and there was a sea of possibilities at their feet. They were still young enough to wade around in the shallows, experiment with life a bit before treading into the depths.

Josh tapped a column of ash onto the rocks. Lily lifted her feet and criss-crossed her legs on the bench, grossed out by the isopods that crawled among the stones. Though the bugs were harder to spot at night, they were also much more prevalent.

Smiling at his wife, Josh flinched when the cloud from her mouth cleared. Lily noticed.

"What?" she said, then immediately glanced over her shoulder. "Oh, no. Josh?"

"Don't worry, Lil. It's fine. We can't stop the guy from walking on the beach."

"But we can leave."

"These cigars weren't cheap. We can't bring them into the pension. Let's just—" With a stunted gasp, Josh went quiet.

"What? Josh? You're freaking me out."

"Look at how fast he's moving…"

Now that the man had stepped away from the lampposts, he was reduced to a giant dark shape among shadows. He wasn't running, but he was moving toward them with a great deal more haste than a tired old fisherman on his way home.

With the tide at its peak, the stone beach did not stretch back very far. This made it difficult to determine whether the man was actually heading for them or simply moving in their general direction. If he really was strolling the length of the beach, he would still have to pass within a few meters of them.

"Stay here," said Josh. He chugged the rest of his beer and plugged the cigar into his mouth like an Old West sheriff.

"Josh!" Lily hissed. "What are you—"

"Just stay here!"

He walked unsteadily atop the rocks. They clacked and wobbled with each step. Though he wanted to present a sturdy, intimidating frame to the approaching stranger, he kept having to look down and test the integrity of the stones below. A sprained ankle would do him no good in a fight.

As the man neared, Josh got a better sense of his size. He had to be almost six and a half feet tall and built like a fucking prize-winning steer. He was maybe thirty or forty meters away, but his pace had increased. His arms now swung in a light jog.

Josh glanced back at Lily. She'd put down her cigar and was frantically searching for her phone.

"Hello, sir!" Josh called out in Korean, raising one hand and puffing out his chest. A stone tilted under his right foot. Maintaining his balance stretched his calf painfully. His ankle joint popped. Instead of continuing, he planted his feet and held his hand out in the international sign for *Stop Right There.*

A large wave crashed on the shore, spraying Josh's cheek. Lily yelped behind him. The stranger grunted like a hog, his trajectory undoubtedly honed in on Josh.

"Josh! Let's go!"

"Stay there, Lil. Give me some light."

Twenty meters.

Lily turned on her phone's flashlight and aimed it at Josh's back. It barely made a dent in the seaside darkness. Without thinking, she stood up and darted forward, holding out her phone in an attempt to illuminate the man's face. All it did was accentuate the shadows.

Then, for an instant, the light hit the stranger in a way that allowed them both a brief glimpse. His features were regular enough—graying stubble, sun-darkened skin, close-cropped hair, a scar on one cheek that probably came from a fishing hook—but his expression was twisted by animalistic rage. His eyes were slits of hatred, drilling through Josh.

The man's murderous scowl spooked Lily, who was now just a few steps behind Josh, and she dropped her phone.

What little light they had vanished.

"Lil, get out of here."

"What? I'm not—"

"Run! Now!"

Lily took off toward the concrete stairway leading up to the road and the pensions. Almost at once, her foot slipped into a crack between two stones, twisting her ankle and splaying her onto the rocks.

Five meters. Close enough for Josh to detect the overpowering stench of fish.

"Get up, Lily! Hurry up!" Josh had glanced back for only a second when he heard her fall. He immediately turned back, stepping forward to block the beastly man from his wife. "Hey! Leave us alone! I said back off, asshole!"

The man did not display the slightest reaction, so Josh dropped into an athletic stance, lowering his shoulder and charging at the guy.

When Lily tried to get to her feet, flaming pain tore through her ankle. She tried to scramble away on her belly, but the stones shifted as she pulled herself. She had no choice but to stand up. As she did, she brought a hefty stone with her, clutching it below her chin.

Hoping to tackle him, Josh ground his shoulder into the man's abdomen, driving upward with his hips. It was like a stubborn Kia playing chicken with a freight train. As they collided, the man bent low, looping his arms underneath Josh's and lifting him clear off the ground.

Lily screamed as Josh careened through the air. He landed hard on the picnic table, his spine bending unnaturally over the edge. And the man, his momentum unaffected, continued after Josh, who was groaning and struggling to crawl underneath the table. The man grabbed Josh by the leg, a giant hand wrapping fully around his ankle, and hauled him away. He didn't drag him far, just far enough so that the picnic table wouldn't interfere. He dropped Josh, stood up to his full, massive height, and prepared to bring two crushing fists down on Josh's head.

Hobbling on her injured leg, it took Lily a while to cover

the distance. The man seemed to have forgotten about her, or was simply uninterested. Even though the rocks shifted beneath her feet and her ragged breaths mingled with her terrified wheezing, he didn't seem to hear her approaching. She made sure she had a firm grip on the rock and favored her uninjured ankle. When she came within striking distance, she lunged at him, swinging the rock with two hands, aiming for his spine.

She managed to hit roughly where she meant to, on the lower neck. The rock hit bone and bounced from her hands. To avoid it crushing her foot, she leapt aside, wincing at the stabbing pain in her bad ankle.

For a moment, it seemed to have worked. She'd hit the man before he landed another blow on Josh. However, he did not fall to his knees or go unconscious. He didn't even stagger. Instead, he turned and glared at Lily. He muttered something she couldn't understand. It was Korean, but his dialect was unlike any she had ever heard.

He made a sudden motion as though to reach out and grab or strike her. Lily responded with a shrieking scream at the top of her lungs. Everyone still awake in the beachfront pensions would have heard her. Someone would come out to help. Hopefully, they'd come quickly.

Never taking her eyes off the man, and continuing to scream as long as her lungs held out, Lily bent over for another stone.

The man chuckled when she hurled it at him, a low laugh, menacing yet somehow playful. He caught the rock with one hand, like a tennis ball, then fell upon her before she could even pivot away.

The rock struck her between the eyes. She felt her nose break. Warm blood rained down her face, filling her mouth. Her ears were ringing so loudly she could no longer hear the surf against the stones. But she did hear, faintly, Josh calling her name.

"Lily... Lily... No... Leave her alone... Lily..."

Josh's vision was blurry as he watched the man gather their things from the picnic table. The beer cans, their phones, Josh's Hawaiian shirt, and Lily's beach hat all went into the tote bag. Josh couldn't move. The wind had been knocked out of him, and he'd heard something snap in his back when he landed on the picnic table. All he could do was mutter weakly, trying to talk some reason into this lunatic slinging their tote bag over his shoulder. Their novelty tote with an owl printed on the side. The owl had squinty eyes and a puckered beak, with a speech bubble that read *Whoooo...are you looking at?* Josh and Lily took the bag everywhere, but it looked ridiculous slung over this man's shoulder.

A few lights came on up at the pensions. A window or two may have briefly opened, but nobody came out to investigate the short-lived screams.

Seeing that Josh was still alert and trying to crawl toward Lily, the man slowly approached. He placed the toe of his boot on Josh's windpipe and applied pressure until Josh lost consciousness.

Lily came to a few minutes later. She was disoriented and nauseous. Her eyes wouldn't focus. It felt like she was being carried somewhere. After blinking two dozen times, her eyes began to clear.

She was on her side, slung over a shoulder. Josh was

unconscious and draped over the other shoulder. A pallid orange glow lit her husband's face from above, his shadowy features shifting as they lumbered along. They were no longer on the beach, but she didn't know where they were.

Yes, she did know.

The orange lights.

They were on the pier.

When the man dropped them a moment later, the ground swayed unsteadily. The world rocked like a giant cradle, the smell of rotten fish coiled around her stomach, and the sound of the surf was replaced by waves slapping the hull below.

2

THE CAULDWELL CHILDREN had been so elated about the summer trip that anyone uninformed might have guessed they were spending the week at Disneyland. For Gina and Helix, Geoje Island was just as good. Being on vacation seemed to have given them an endless reservoir of energy, and they rose at ungodly hours. Ron and Jane just barely managed to keep up. Exhausted from waking at the crack of dawn every day, they started going to bed early with the kids, leaving their childless friends, Josh and Lily, to drink the nights away on their own.

There weren't many options to keep the little sprites occupied at 5:30 AM. They had packed plenty of toys and games, but the children were uninterested. They wanted to go out. Anywhere. To the beach, the shipbuilding yards, the interior mountains, the smaller surrounding islands, even the old

POW camp that had been turned into a kind of grim amusement park.

Only one thing could temporarily strangle their attention while mom and dad eased into the new day with instant coffee, yawns, and lukewarm showers. *The Little Mermaid.* This was more Gina's obsession than Helix's, but Helix was at that age where he wanted to emulate everything his older sister did.

Stretched out in front of Jane's iPad, Gina bellowed along to the songs and Helix crooned like a dying cat. They made it through the movie once, became restless, then started it again from the beginning. Right around the second time the prince fell under the sea witch's spell, their parents were finally ready to head out.

"Aunt Lily, *come on!*" cried Gina as her dad gently knocked on the door to Josh and Lily's room.

"I'm sure they're still sleeping, sweetie." Ron nudged Gina away before she started pounding on the door and woke the whole pension. "Not everyone likes to get up with the sun like you do."

"But we're on va-*cation*," complained Gina. "We have to *do stuff!*"

"We have to let them sleep or they'll be too grumpy to play with you at the beach this afternoon."

This seemed to pacify Gina. She ran down the stairs to find her mother and brother outside. Ron trailed behind, typing out a text message to Josh.

The cafe across the street served simple breakfast sets. More importantly, they brewed real coffee. Ron and Jane were tired of the instant stuff and watered-down Americanos.

The kids ate quickly, and it wasn't long before they were

bouncing off the walls. Helix kept standing on his chair, nearly tipping it over backwards. Gina wanted to play with the owner's golden lab, but the dog just lay in its corner. The woman explained that the dog was sixteen years old and didn't do much anymore, which drew a pitying look from Gina. When they could no longer restrain the children, they headed across the road and down the concrete stairs to Mangchi Mongdol Beach.

They stopped at the convenience store for juice and snacks for the kids. While Ron and Jane settled in around one of the picnic tables, Gina and Helix went directly for the water.

The beach wasn't very good for swimming, and the kids weren't wearing their bathing suits. They waded around in the shallows, Gina holding Helix's hand and pointing out fish. Every once in a while, she belted out a lyric from *The Little Mermaid*. Helix became infatuated with the isopods crawling over the rocks. He kept trying to catch them, eliciting yelps of disgust from his sister and laughter from his parents.

"How hard is it to clean up after yourself?" grumbled Jane.

Ever the neat-freak, she kept glaring at the picnic table two down from theirs, where an inconsiderate bunch had left their trash. She became so incensed that she went to clean up the mess herself. She gathered the empty beer cans, dumped out the leftover soup from the cup noodles, crumpled the spent prawn chip wrappers, and picked up red-stained chopsticks from the rocks. She shoved it all into the plastic bag from the convenience store and neatly tied it off.

"I'm going to look for a trash can. Keep an eye on the kids?"

"I was thinking I might sneak off to the pub for a few."

"Very funny."

"Hurry back, love."

While Jane was gone, Ron helped the kids build a stone tower. They successfully stacked eight stones, then started building a fortification wall around it when Helix got it into his head to launch a rock missile, demolishing their progress. The tower fell, and it looked like Gina was about to cry. Just as Ron knelt down to console her, she started laughing hysterically. She and Helix then built a second tower with the sole intention of knocking it down.

"Ronnie, come over here."

Jane was standing by the picnic table on the end, staring at the rocks.

"What is it, babe?"

She pointed underneath the table at a half-smoked cigar butt wedged between stones. Ron squatted down and reached under the seat. The cigar still smelled fresh, if not a little salty.

"Do you think it's theirs?" asked Jane.

Ron groaned as he stood up, then shrugged. "Probably. I doubt too many others are smoking these things by the beach."

Jane scanned the rocks around the picnic table, a worried look on her face. Ron examined the cigar band.

"Damn, Josh went all out with these."

"What?"

"This is a hundred-dollar cigar. Why the hell would they waste half of it?"

Jane's eyes suddenly went wide. "Did you hear screaming last night?"

Ron considered for a moment. "Maybe. I was out like the

dead, but...I heard something. I guess I assumed they were fucking."

"Me, too..." Jane grimaced. "But now that I think of it, it sounded like the screams came from outside."

"So they were fucking on the beach. Why not? We've done it. Remember in—"

"It wasn't that kind of scream, Ron."

"Then they were fighting." Ron shrugged. "Finally had the blowout you were expecting. Maybe we shouldn't have closed the pool after the wedding."

"Yeah, maybe..."

Gina came running over, squealing and giggling madly. Helix had finally caught one of the isopods and was chasing her with it. They ran circles around the picnic table where their parents were talking. Finally, Gina hid behind Jane's leg and demanded Helix drop the revolting critter. Helix complied, though his attention span was about as long as a puppy's and he instantly tried to catch it again.

"Dad-*dy!* What is *that?*" squealed Gina, pointing at the cigar.

"Just some trash, sweetie. Real expensive trash."

"Did they come to the door when you knocked?" asked Jane.

Ron shook his head, then took out his phone. "And Josh hasn't replied to my text yet. Don't worry. They probably got hammered and had at it. Now they're hungover. Let them sleep it off. They won't even remember what they were fighting about."

Jane thought he was probably right. Still, she brought out her phone and dialed Lily.

"No answer."

"They'll get in touch when they wake up. Maybe they want a day to themselves. We can't expect them to put up with the kids all week."

"Hey!" shouted Gina gleefully. "Where did Helix get *paint?*"

Ron and Jane stared at their daughter in confusion. They turned to Helix, who was sitting on the rocks and playing with one particularly large stone. His hands were smeared with red. Ron thought it might be some kind of algae.

"Hey, buddy. Bring that here."

Happily, Helix lugged the stone over to his dad. Ron shoved the cigar into his breast pocket and held up the rock, peering at the drippy, red substance.

It sure as hell wasn't paint or algae.

"Hmm..."

"What is it?" Jane stepped closer, craning her neck.

"I think it's blood."

Jane's face went ashen. Helix had lost interest and suddenly ran to the water's edge. A fishing boat was slowly chugging toward the pier at the end of the beach.

"Boat!" announced Helix.

"Gina," said Ron. "Go and watch your brother. Make him rinse his hands, and don't let him go into the water alone."

The girl bounded after Helix, reciting some line from the movie. "'*It's a dinglehopper! It's a dinglehopper!*'"

"Ron," Jane whispered. "What are we going to do?"

"What do you mean? We don't even know if it's theirs. There were plenty of other people down here last night, and it's hard to walk on these stupid rocks. Anyone could twist an ankle or scrape a knee or bash their head."

Jane crossed her arms and turned around, gazing up the hill at their pension.

"I think we should check on them."

"It's not even ten o'clock, Janie. They haven't gotten up this early the entire trip."

"But—"

"When they do straggle out of bed, we'll talk to them. Okay? I'm sure everything's fine."

"Boat! Boat!"

"Poor, unfortunate souls!" Gina cackled in perfect mimicry of the sea witch.

Ron and Jane both turned to watch the kids. Gina was holding Helix by the wrist as he pointed at the incoming fishing boat and splashed in the shallows. Jane kept sighing. Ron put his arm around her, but she immediately wriggled out of his embrace.

"Look, Janie. Just send Lily a message. Explain that we're worried. You know how attached she is to her phone. Probably sleeps with it in her hand."

Ron watched the boat angling into an empty spot on the pier. Jane stared out to sea. Across the bay, people were arriving at Gujora Beach. They walked along the sand in colorful swimsuits, choosing parasols to rent for the day. Inner tubes appeared on the water. Occasionally, the shrill screech of a lifeguard's whistle carried all the way to Mangchi Mongdol.

A rowdy group came down the steps from the road. It looked like four generations of a family, from the matronly grannie down to a couple of great-grandchildren about Gina's age. They stayed away from the picnic tables, laying a large mat over the stones instead.

Gina turned to watch the family while she held onto Helix. Her brother was so captivated by the boat that he hadn't even noticed the newcomers. She kept having to reassert her grip on his wet wrist.

Jane pulled out her phone again and opened her message thread with Lily.

Ron stared at the bloody stone. Though he tried not to show it, he felt the gaping emptiness of anxiety hollowing his stomach. He did believe that Josh and Lily were fine—most likely hungover and quite possibly not speaking to one another—but he couldn't deny that there was something disquieting about the blood. And he knew Josh. Josh would never, ever, *ever* allow a hundred-dollar cigar to go to waste.

"Helix! Come *back!*"

When Ron and Jane looked up, their son was already a good way down the beach. Gina ran after him, but she had a hard time negotiating the rocks. After a dozen steps, she tripped, wailing as she sprawled forward while Helix scampered off toward the pier.

Like his daughter, Ron did not have the easiest time walking over the stones. He let his wife run after Helix while he checked on Gina. She was crying, not from the scrapes on her hands and knees but because she'd let her brother get away. With difficulty, she tried to explain that she'd become distracted, but Ron couldn't make heads or tails of her wheezing speech. Finally, she pointed toward the family down the beach.

"What about them, honey?"

"There!" She was gesturing into the water where one of the children was perched on an inner tube in the shape of a crab. "It's *Sebastian!*"

Ron got Gina to her feet, wiping away her tears and pointing toward Jane and Helix. The boy was in his mother's arms, and they were headed back, but Ron was shocked to see how far Helix had made it before Jane caught him. And Helix was evidently unhappy about being stopped. He was crying with an intensity they rarely heard from the usually placid child.

While waiting for Jane and Helix, Ron studied the vessel that had drawn his son away. A mid-sized boat, bigger than some of the others moored along the pier. The hull was painted rust red with the name written in large golden letters. *Sea of Run*. Or was it *Ruin*? A moderate cabin bulged at the center. The owner had just finished tying it off and was now climbing onto the pier. An enormous man, by the looks of it. He lumbered along with the stooped gait characteristic of all oversized individuals.

Jane arrived with Helix still reaching over her shoulder toward the pier. Though the boy kept murmuring about the boat, his crying had waned.

Ron took the boy from her, turning to allow him a clear view of the vessel. He spoke to his son, commenting on the boat's unique features, explaining its purpose, hopefully satiating some of the boy's curiosity. Jane had begun to lightly scold Gina, but she trailed off almost at once, recognizing that they could not blame their six-year-old for such an innocent mistake.

The fisherman made it to the end of the pier and stopped at the stairs leading down to the beach. Hands on his hips, he stared over the waterfront. Ron pointed him out to Helix, saying that was the man who drove the boat and caught the fish.

After a minute, when both kids had calmed down, they all returned to the picnic table. Gina was still throwing interested glances at the inner tube. The grandfather was in the water playing with the two young children, and the rest of the family was munching on roasted squid and sipping soju. A few other groups were wandering down from the pensions. Jane watched hopefully, but Josh and Lily were not among them.

Ron and Jane sat the kids at the picnic table. Helix, still restless, immediately stood on the seat to dig through the snacks they'd brought. Gina gazed wistfully at the sea. Ron knew the look in his daughter's eyes—she wanted to go and play with the kids in the water. She was an outgoing child who, having been raised in Korea, was quite confident in her ability to communicate. However, Ron assumed she felt bad about letting Helix get away, making her hesitant to ask if she could join them.

Jane finished her text to Lily, Ron checked his phone for a message from Josh, and Helix was trying to open a package of gummy worms.

"If we don't hear from them soon," Ron said, turning away from the kids and speaking low, "why don't we take a ferry to one of the smaller islands? Might be a nice change of pace."

"Don't you think Josh and Lil would want to join us?"

"Well, yeah...but they can't expect us to wait around all morning like this. Every day. I expect it will continue. And... we could probably all use a break from each other."

Jane stared at her phone as though expecting a reply from Lily at any second. She sighed. "I suppose so, but..."

"But what?"

"I'm worried, Ron."

"Fish man!" Helix beamed, a blue and pink worm hanging from his teeth. Ron and Jane both gave tense smiles.

"I know you are," said Ron, lowering his voice further still. "But they're fine. What could have happened to them?"

An eruption of laughter came from the Korean family. The old lady was relating some story that had the younger ones rolling around on the rocks.

"Was their car still there?" asked Jane abruptly.

"Josh and Lily's? Yeah, I think so."

"I want to go and check on them."

"Janie... If they got into an argument, maybe they don't want to be disturbed. Let's just give them some space. When they're ready, they'll—"

"Fish man!" Helix repeated. He was pointing toward the pier. Ron glanced up.

"What's he talking about?" muttered Jane, glancing over her shoulder.

The fisherman was plodding along the stones, already about halfway down the beach, coming in their direction. The man appeared to be in his fifties, probably closer to sixty, and bigger than just about any Korean Ron had ever seen. He wore a baggy gray fishing bib, which made it difficult to determine his precise size. He was neither fat nor muscular, but had a thick, solid build. The shoulders and arms of a heavyweight boxer. Beneath his grizzled stubble, his features were chiseled, his flesh darkened by years under the sun, and his hair cropped close. A long scar stretched from his nose to his left earlobe. Like most Korean men his age, he bore no expression but only stared straight ahead with a slightly annoyed scowl.

As the fisherman passed by the picnic table on the end,

where they'd found the cigar, he paused, peering as though he'd spotted something.

Since there was plenty of room for him to go around, it seemed odd that the man was walking straight at them. His blatant staring, though unsettling, was not entirely uncommon. In the rural parts of Korea, it was normal for people, especially older folks, to stare at a white family. However, when the man abruptly stopped beside their picnic table, observing them with peculiar intensity, Jane shivered and glanced nervously at the kids.

"Hello," said Ron, standing to greet him.

Gina watched with interest.

Helix stood on the bench again. "Fish man!"

The man looked sharply at Helix. A great smile extended across his face, bringing out his dimples and crow's feet. "Fish man!" he repeated in a deep voice, his accent so thick it sounded like he said *Pee Cee-ment*.

They all had a good laugh at this. Ron tried to apologize, but the man brushed it off, explaining in his heavily accented English that he'd actually come to apologize to them. From the pier, he'd seen the boy run off toward the boat.

"Boat!" yelled Helix excitedly, bringing on another round of laughter. This piqued Gina's interest. She had been so distracted by the inner tube shaped like a cartoon crab that she'd hardly noticed why Helix ran away. Now, she stood up and came around to her mother's side, gazing at the moored boats.

"Which one?" Gina asked.

The fisherman squatted to her level and pointed. "Dat boat. Red boat."

"I see it!" Gina exclaimed. "Sea of Run!"

"Right," he smiled. "Sea of Ruin."

A squealed greeting came from the family on the mat. The old woman was looking at them and waving, speaking to the fisherman in an unintelligible island dialect. He excused himself, jogging over to the family, where he bowed deeply to the old lady and greeted the others. They spoke for a few minutes, an animated, noisy conversation punctuated by laughter and the repeated use of honorific speech.

Ron suggested they drive over to Gujora Beach so the kids could swim. Jane agreed and began gathering their things. They would have to stop at their room to change into swimsuits, and they could knock on Josh and Lily's door again while they were there.

"You go?" The fisherman returned, a warm, broad smile on his lips. His cheeks seemed rosier after his interaction with the old woman.

"Yes," nodded Ron. "We thought we might head over to Gujora."

"Are they friends of yours?" asked Jane, indicating the Korean family.

The fisherman smiled. "I know Mrs Park forty year. She… buy *pee-shee*."

"Computers?" asked Gina.

The fisherman rumbled with laughter.

"I think he means *fish*, sweetie," said Ron, blushing.

"Fish man!" howled Helix, growing excited again. He started jumping around, nearly losing his balance on the wobbly rocks. "Boat! Boat! Boat!"

"You want go to boat?" asked the fisherman, grinning at the boy.

"Helix, leave the nice man alone," said Jane, checking her phone.

But both Helix and Gina were nodding enthusiastically. The mere idea of it made them gaze longingly at the water.

"I take you," suggested the man, seemingly delighted by the idea.

Ron made eye contact with Jane and shrugged. "It could be fun. The kids have never been on a boat."

"I don't know, Ron..." said Jane nervously. "It's dangerous."

The fisherman threw his head back, laughing. Helix saw this and mimicked him.

"Danger, no," said the fisherman. He gestured at the bay, trying to convey that the water was perfectly flat. "Please, you come. Short trip. Go island?"

"We were hoping to visit one of the smaller islands..." said Ron. They'd been to the beach every day of the trip so far. He was itching to do something different, and he didn't really want to deal with the problem of Josh and Lily anymore. The more he thought about it, the more it seemed like a good idea. "We could pay you."

"Island, I know. No pay. Gift, for trouble."

"What trouble?" asked Ron.

"The boy. He...run."

"Does your boat have life vests and preservers?" asked Jane.

The fisherman stared at her dumbly, clearly not understanding. Ron didn't know the Korean word for *life vest*, so he mimed wearing a bulky vest and strung together a series of Korean words that meant *safety floating shirt*.

This, the man understood and began trying to explain, in a blend of languages, that he sometimes took Mrs Park's great-grandchildren out on the water, so the boat had vests and even a few child-sized fishing rods.

While Ron squatted down to speak to the kids, Jane stared uncomfortably at the fisherman. On the side of his fishing bib, underneath his armpit, she noticed a red clump stuck to the hem. It was wet, shiny, organic. The man noticed her looking and smiled.

"*Pee-shee*, clean and..." he offered as an explanation, but couldn't find the right words. Glancing down to make sure the kids weren't looking, he mimed hacking off a fish's head.

"I see," Jane gave a tight smile. "Ron, I think we should just—"

"Boat! Boat! Boat!" the kids interrupted, chanting with conviction now.

Ron stood up and looked at her. "Sorry. I think they're already set on it. It'll be fun, Janie."

It took a few more minutes for Jane to be swayed. Ron never would have convinced her by himself, but the prospect of an unexpected boat ride had lifted the children to a rapturous fervor. Jane saw their smiles, their bright, pleading eyes, and there was no way she could refuse. The fisherman, who eventually introduced himself as Mr Moon, wasn't pretty on the eyes, but he seemed like a harmless, jolly old man.

And while Jane was still worried about Josh and Lily, she knew Ron was right. At best, those two had a rocky relationship. Both temperamental, flighty, and prone to jealousy. It was a miracle they were still together after a year of marriage. Although, when things were good between them, they were really good. It was not out of the question that they'd stayed up all night fucking and were still at it, a thought that made Jane flutter with envy.

The Cauldwells gathered their things, Mr Moon said goodbye to Mrs Park and her family, and they all headed for the pier. While they walked, Mr Moon asked the kids what they thought of his home island, impressed beyond measure when they answered in Korean. He went on to explain that Mrs Park ran a seafood restaurant near Gujora Beach and had been buying fish from him for years. Having grown up in Geoje, he had always been a fisherman, but it wasn't his livelihood. He had worked at the shipyards for thirty-five years, throughout the period of Korea's rise to dominance in the shipbuilding industry. After retirement, he spent most of his time out on his boat, catching mackerel, hairtail, sea bass, and flatfish. Sometimes, he simply stared out at the water, reflecting on the fortunate tranquility of his waning years.

"The name of your boat?" said Ron as they mounted the pier. "What does it mean?"

"It mean, hmm...how to say... Flow of life. To death."

"Sea of *Run*? Like running a race?"

"Yes, right. Sea of Ruin."

Gina heard them talking and started singing *Under the Sea.* Jane was holding Helix's hand, and he pulled her ahead, staring in fascination at every boat they passed. When they reached Mr Moon's vessel, he asked them to wait on the pier while he prepared it. He hopped on, pulled up a bucketful of seawater, and splashed it over the deck. Dark red water drained from the scuppers. Jane cringed at the sight, thinking again about the bit of bloody flesh stuck to the man's bib.

Mr Moon apologized for the mess, explaining that he'd had a successful night's fishing.

Ron boarded first, taking Helix from Jane and then helping Gina. Mr Moon offered his hand to Jane. She took it reluctantly, wishing she had stood her ground and refused this little journey, even at the risk of letting down the kids. Once she was standing on the deck, her reservations only increased.

Boating gear lay scattered everywhere. Fishing rods, nets, gaffs, buckets. Empty beer and soju bottles. More equipment was mounted on the wall inside the cabin. Knives, hatchets, a machete, and a mallet. Traces of fish matter clung to the floor near the scuppers. Scales, tails, fins, and guts. The overpowering stench of fish seemed baked into the wood and plastic.

"Ron...?" Jane hissed.

He turned to her, smiling, and instantly recognized the look on her face.

"It's fine, Janie. Good for the kids."

"How?"

"It's authentic. Not some sterile ferry. They'll remember this. Just try to relax and have a good time."

Mr Moon had pulled out the life vests. The two small ones fit the kids snugly. Ron was a strong swimmer, so he didn't take one. Jane, already feeling nauseous before they embarked, did. Mr Moon cleared off the benches at the bow and wiped them down with a wet rag. Once the family was settled in, he untied from the pier and started the engine.

As they slowly swung around, redirecting out to sea, Helix grew silent with awe. Seagulls circled overhead, mewing and squealing. Gina leaned over the rail, staring into the water, pointing out the occasional fish. The hull rumbled beneath them, bouncing gently along the tranquil waters. Beyond the bay, the waves were larger but still relatively calm.

"How far are we going?" Jane asked Ron uneasily.

"He said the island is nearby. Maybe fifteen minutes?"

"Go and ask him, Ron. If it's any longer than that, I don't think we should."

Ron glanced at the kids, who were having the time of their lives. He was about to say something, but just nodded and got up. He went into the cabin with Mr Moon.

The man smiled and waved Ron over, gesturing at the controls. "You drive."

Ron tried to protest, but Mr Moon grabbed him by the shoulders and set him at the helm. He pointed straight ahead, where the bay opened onto the sea. Once Ron got the hang of it, Mr Moon stepped to the side and attempted to explain the boat's controls.

"You smoke big cigar," stated Mr Moon, a curious drawl to his words.

"I'm sorry?"

Mr Moon tapped Ron's breast pocket. The burnt end of the cigar stuck up like a scorched thumb.

"Oh," Ron laughed. "Yes, sometimes."

"Last night, I meet other. Foreign smoker."

"Did you? On the beach?"

Mr Moon nodded, then reached out to correct Ron's course.

"They must have been our friends. Did you speak to them?"

"No speak."

"Were they fighting, by any chance? We haven't heard from them this morning. We think they might have gotten into an argument. They do that sometimes. An emotional couple."

"Yes. Fight."

Ron chuckled and nodded. "I knew it. How far is this

island, Mr Moon? We don't want to take up too much of your day."

"Not far. Twenty minute. First, children fish. Good fishing. Drive straight, ten minute."

Mr Moon went out onto the bow to talk with Jane and the kids. Gina and Helix laughed wildly when he showed them how to feed the seagulls that followed the boat.

It was harder than Ron thought to keep a straight course. He did the best he could, but he was distracted, watching his kids laugh and circulate around the deck as Mr Moon prepared the fishing rods and bait. Jane, however, wasn't looking so good. Pale as a ghost, she leaned forward with her head near her knees, unwilling to take her eyes off the kids even though it looked like she might be sick at the next wave.

"Shit," muttered Ron. He wanted to go to her, but he couldn't just leave the helm unmanned. He looked around, trying to decipher what was what, and saw, for the first time, that the interior of the cabin was filthy. The floor was caked with grime and blood and fish guts. Mold grew in the corners, splatters of what looked like mud hung from the walls, and a film covered the windows. Strangely, the smell of fish was not as powerful as it was on the deck. When Ron brought his hands off the controls, a sticky coating clung to his fingers, the dark stains of unwashed years.

So much water and yet so unclean.

Mr Moon finished preparing the rods and came into the cabin to shut off the engine. He led Ron back onto the bow.

"Dis place, many *pee-shee*." He pointed out a small, rocky island with few trees. "Island is...no people. Peace."

"Where are all the other boats?" asked Jane.

"*Pee-shee* come early morning and...sun sink." He pointed upward, shielding his eyes. "Sun bad for *pee-shee*."

The boat bobbed in the waves about halfway between the bay and the tiny island. When Jane saw that the island was close, she seemed to relax, though she still looked sick. Ron sat down next to her while Mr Moon helped the children put their lines in the water.

"Are you feeling alright?" asked Ron.

Jane shook her head. "I think I'm going to throw up."

"That's weird. You've never gotten seasick before, have you?"

"I don't think it's the water. Maybe the smell or..."

"What?"

"Something just feels...wrong."

"Why don't you go into the cabin. It's not pretty, but it doesn't smell so bad in there. You can lie down. If it doesn't pass, I'll tell him to take us back after fishing."

Ron led Jane inside. He cleared off the long, matted bench, wiped it down with an old, soiled rag, and got her situated.

"Close your eyes," he said. "Take deep breaths. Drink some water. I'll be out with the kids. Give a shout if you need to puke."

To Jane's surprise, it worked. Though the cabin was stuffy, damp, and thick with the odor of engine oil, it smelled significantly less of fish. The boat rocked gently atop the waves, like the comforting sway of a hammock. A few sips of water from the bottle in her purse helped to soothe her stomach. The sweat on her brow dried, her head cleared, and the sound of her children hooting and hollering on the bow made her smile. She figured she'd just rest until they got to the island.

She didn't need to see any flopping fish with bloodied hooks through their mouths, and she wasn't entirely sure how the kids would handle it. Hopefully, they would understand and Mr Moon would toss the fish back.

Opening her eyes, she gazed at the ceiling. It was splattered with dark stains. She didn't know a thing about cleaning fish and could not fathom how blood might spray the entire cabin. Jane leaned up on her elbows. Out on the deck, Mr Moon was giving Gina tips. Ron knelt beside Helix, helping him hold the rod. She was glad the kids were having fun, but that didn't stop her from wishing this little adventure would end.

Lying back, Jane wondered how anyone could live like this, in almost constant solitude, dedicated to hunting and killing defenseless creatures, literally surrounded by the gory remains of the catch. It seemed such a macabre, nightmarish way to live. Clearly, the old man was lonely. Why else would he have invited a family of strangers he could barely communicate with onto his boat?

On the wall behind her hung a small collection of knives. The largest was the machete; the smallest resembled a fruit knife, perilously sharp. In one corner was something that looked like an oversized umbrella holder. It contained numerous fishing rods and gaffs. The rusty hooks and spears made Jane shiver. All of these tools displayed traces of recent use. Brownish stains colored the steel blades. Dried, crusted remnants of scales and flesh caked the handles and sharp edges. From a few, red droplets trailed down. A dark puddle had formed beneath the gaffs, and it looked relatively fresh.

Now that the boat wasn't moving, it might be alright to go back onto the deck, see how the kids were getting along, maybe urge them to wrap it up. But the smell on deck was sure to make her retch. And they were still squealing with laughter. She didn't want to ruin it for them.

Gina suddenly yelped with delight. "I got one!"

Then, from Ron, "We do, too!"

"Fish man!" beamed Helix.

"Is big! Dis way, follow *pee-shee!*" Mr Moon directed Gina along the port side to the aft, trailing the fish's lead. "You can?" he said to Ron.

"No problem! I got it! You help Gina!"

Their laughter and babble increased as the two pairs attempted to reel in their catches. Jane smiled and lay back. She took out her phone, wondering if there would be any reception out here. They were maybe a kilometer off the coast.

Her phone had two bars. Lily had not yet responded to the message. Jane tapped Lily's contact info and dialed her number. It rang and rang, unanswered. On the deck, they had quieted down, focused on the task of hauling in their prizes.

A familiar sound startled Jane.

Buzzing.

She didn't just hear it; she felt it.

Vibrating.

She checked her purse, thinking that maybe Ron had slipped his phone there for safekeeping. It wasn't there, and when she looked out the window, she saw Ron taking a selfie of himself and Helix. She looked around but didn't see a phone that might belong to Mr Moon. And, the vibrations seemed to be coming from directly below her. Underneath the bench.

Jane ran her fingers along the mat, discovering that it was

not attached. When she slid it aside, she saw that the wooden bench was also a storage cabinet.

She lifted the lid and stared, dumbfounded by what was inside.

Whoooo...are you looking at?

"Ron..."

On the bow, Ron had Helix in his arms. Helix held the rod while Ron reeled it in.

At the stern, Gina screamed with glee as Mr Moon shouted, "Pull! Pull!"

Impossible. An idiotic, novelty tote bag like that—there was no way a guy like Mr Moon had the exact same bag. It had to be Josh and Lily's.

Jane looked at her phone. It was still ringing, and she still heard the faint, recognizable sound of a phone set to vibrate. It was coming from the owl bag. Her heart seemed to stop. A lump formed in her throat. She felt nauseous again as she peeked out the back. Mr Moon was stooped over her daughter like an ogre, encouraging her as he reached into the water with a fishing net.

The tote bag didn't contain much. Jane dug around until she found the vibrating phone.

She pulled it out, shaking her head at Lily's unmistakable anime phone case. And on the screen—

Incoming Call: Jane.

She ended the call.

Dread and panic began to radiate from her skin like a flash fever.

A spiderweb crack cut across Lily's phone screen. At dinner the night before, when Lily had been sharing videos from the beach, the screen had been undamaged.

"Ron…"

All she could manage was a whisper. She could hardly breathe. Setting down the two phones, she searched through the tote bag. Two empty cans of beer and two unopened ones. Josh's Hawaiian shirt. A cigar cutter. Lily's sunhat. Another half-smoked cigar.

"Ron…"

Louder this time. She scanned the cabin, her eyes wide and unblinking. Details she'd noticed before now carried new, frightening implications. The blood-stained knives. The puddle beneath the gaffs. The splatters on the ceiling. The thick, clotted stains in the corners and on the floor. The entire boat painted a sinister hue. And the smell was not just of fish but almost like being in a butcher shop.

Out the windows, the sea rose and fell around them. They were too far out to swim to shore. No other boats were visible on these waters.

"Got him!" yelled Ron. "Look at that, buddy! Almost as big as you!"

"Fish man! Fish man!"

"Ron…"

"Scoop it, Mr Moon! Scoop it! Don't hurt it!"

"Hold! Strong girl! Hold!"

"*RON!*"

Silence descended. Everyone held their breath. Even the wind receded. The only sound was the rolling waves slapping the hull.

Ron handed the rod and line to Helix, then he hurried into the cabin. Jane was pale again, paler than before. She held up a tote bag he recognized at once.

"What…?" Ron muttered. Josh and Lily had been carrying the bag around all week.

Tears spilled down Jane's cheeks, and just as Ron went to her, a wet splat sounded behind him. The fish flopped frantically around the deck. Helix fell to his knees to try to catch it.

"Leave it, Helix. I'll be right there…"

Ron wrapped his arms around his wife, muffling her voice against his shoulder.

"They were here," she was saying. "Something happened. Where are they? Why does he have their bag? We have to get off…"

"We're on a boat, Janie. We can't just…"

As he held her, he glanced around the cabin, noting how sticky and wet everything looked. And how *red*.

"Uncle Josh!" shouted Helix.

Breathless, Ron and Jane stared at each other. They ran out to the bow and found Helix kneeling on the deck, staring down into an underfloor storage tank. The hatch opened toward Ron and Jane, so they couldn't see inside. Helix's fish, a two-foot-long sea bass, danced spastically at their feet, but Helix had forgotten all about it. Their son's expression transitioned from elation to frightened bewilderment.

The boy looked up at Ron and Jane. "Aunt Lily's sick?"

Anxiously, their arms wrapped around each other, Ron and Jane scuttled forward to peer into the hole.

Jane screamed.

Ron fell to his knees.

Both Josh and Lily were crammed into the small holding tank. Their bodies were broken, their limbs bent at unnatural angles, their blank eyes gaping at the sky. Lacerations covered their flesh. Blood painted their faces. Lily's nose was shattered.

"No! Stop! *NOOOOO!*" Their daughter's screams, childish at first, rose swiftly until she sounded like a grown woman facing unspeakable horrors.

"Gina!" bawled Jane.

Ron, his senses blurred by reactive panic, leapt to his feet and ran into the cabin. Thinking absently that he ought to find some means of defense, he noticed that the machete no longer hung in its spot on the wall. Instead of reaching for another of the knives, he continued through to the aft, only stopping when a glinting flash of metal swiped past his face.

Gina's screams ended abruptly with a choking, sodden splat.

Jane had picked up Helix and backed to the very tip of the bow. Trembling violently, she put her son down for fear of dropping him and simply buried his face in her thigh. Ron backed out of the cabin and turned to face her, revealing a fine spatter of blood across his stricken face, frozen with an expression of utter disbelief. She'd never seen her husband look so broken.

Heavy footsteps rattled the boat. Ron kept backing up.

Mr Moon ducked through the tiny doorway, emerging from the cabin with a fishing gaff as tall as he was.

Ron dropped to his knees right beside the open lid. His gaze fell upon their dead friends and he vomited. Mr Moon glared at the mess, shaking his head. The spastic fish flopped at his feet. With a sudden, violent stab, he speared the fish's body.

Weeping loudly, Jane tried to shield Helix's eyes from what

was happening, but the immensity of her fear rendered her weak. The boy pried his cheek away from her leg and gasped.

Mr Moon stepped on the sea bass, removed the gaff, and kicked the fish to the side. He gripped the gaff with two hands, lowering it to his side so it was horizontal with the deck. Words tumbled from his mouth, but neither Ron nor Jane could understand him.

Ron pleaded, begged, implored the man to leave his family unharmed.

"Where's Gina? Where's Gina?" blubbered Jane.

"Sissy?" Helix's voice was choked and wet with tears, muffled as his mother buried his face into her thigh again.

The way Mr Moon abruptly narrowed his eyes at Ron made Jane's knees give out. Helix broke out of her grasp, turning around just in time to see Mr Moon shove the gaff forward. The spear pierced Ron straight through the chest, penetrating his back. Flecks of blood landed on Helix's face and Jane's sandaled feet.

Without thinking, Jane lifted Helix and flung him overboard. Helix shrieked in surprise. There was a splash, followed by Helix's spastic cries. Mr Moon ripped the gaff from Ron's body, and Ron fell into a flooding pool of his own blood.

As Mr Moon came forward, he kicked Ron into the fish compartment with Josh and Lily. Jane hopped over the railing into the sea.

"Helix? Helix? *Helix!*"

The current had already dragged the boy several meters away. His head and life vest bounced wildly among the waves, aggravated by his splashing arms.

As Jane started to swim to him, a sudden, sharp pressure

stopped her. She couldn't breathe. The water around her turned crimson and opaque. She felt herself being hauled into the air. And then, nothing.

Mr Moon removed the hook of the gaff from her chest and dropped her body on the deck. Then, he waved to the panicking boy.

"Pee-shee boy! Swim, pee-shee boy! Swim!"

For a long while, the boat bobbed in the waves while Mr Moon stared at the water, appreciating the view of these, his waning years.

A few minutes later, the Sea of Ruin's engine roared to life. The boat chugged away, back toward Mangchi Mongdol Beach, leaving the child to struggle and pray among the waves, the fish, and the ghosts of his family.

Get to the Root of the Problem

For about the fiftieth time since he came home, Drew is having second thoughts about being here. It's only been a week, and he knew it would be a difficult transition, but Jesus Christ, *pulling weeds?* His parents pay a landscaping service for just this kind of thing. So why in the hell is he doing it?

And these goddamn weeds are like steel chains. They look unassuming enough. No different from any other garden weed. Maybe a little more blue-green than green-green. But pulling them out is like trying to rip out a healthy tooth. He tugs and tugs and nothing happens. Finally, something breaks. Drew flops onto his back, heaving and swearing, but it was only the leaves tearing off. The stem still sticks out of the ground, wagging at Drew like a pointed tongue. Examining the long, teardrop-shaped leaves, he notices bright red veins on the underside.

Blueish-green with red highlights?

"Hey, Ma! These things better not be poisonous!" he shouts into the house.

"Put on some gloves, you idiot."

"Why didn't you tell me that?"

"Shouldn't have to remind my grown son about common sense."

A little while later, she comes out on her way to the greenhouse. As she passes by, she looks critically over his shoulder, tut-tutting at his lack of progress. "Wishful thinking," she mutters with a snort.

"What?"

"I thought after five years traipsing around the world you'd have come back with something to show for it. Knowledge? Wisdom? Experience? Isn't that what you claimed to be doing?"

"Yeah, and I was. What I wasn't doing was pulling weeds."

This is a barefaced lie on multiple fronts. During his travels, he had become something of a weed connoisseur. He'd smoked marijuana in every country he passed through, along with a variety of other plant-based drugs. And, more than once, he'd found himself trading labor for lodging. Most of those arrangements were with agricultural families, and he'd been asked to pull weeds from their fields on numerous occasions.

But those weeds always popped right out of the ground. Like the earth knew they were bad news and was just itching to be rid of them.

Here at home, he hasn't unearthed a single plant yet, and now his hands are stinging.

Dozens of tiny scratches crisscross his palms and fingers, some filling with blood. It's the stems. He hadn't noticed, but they're covered in minuscule thorns. He's basically been shredding his hands with fine sandpaper this entire time.

His mom walks by carrying a flowerpot. She sniggers at the sight of his grated hands, then grimaces at the measly pile of leaves.

"Drew. What are you doing?" Exasperation drips from her words. Or is it disappointment?

"What do you mean? I'm—"

"The roots, Drew."

"What?"

"If you only tear off the stems, those weeds will grow back in two days. You have to pull out the roots. You're going to be out here all day at this rate. And I told you to put on some gloves."

"Alright, *alright.*"

The day Drew left for college, he swore he'd never move back into his childhood home, which also happened to be his mother's childhood home. Her parents bought the land back in the fifties when the plots out here on the edge of the expanding city were dirt cheap. Since they intended to raise a large family, they scooped up several adjoining plots to ensure their growing brood would have plenty of space. Drew would have no less than eight aunts and uncles on his mom's side, had they survived. One aunt died during childbirth, losing the child as well. The other two were killed in a car wreck with their boyfriends. All five uncles ended up in Vietnam; only one came back, but he refused to visit his former home. Said it made his PTSD even worse.

So, Drew's mom, at only twenty-one years old, inherited the house when her parents died within days of each other. Complications from an illness that the doctors had never identified. At twenty-six, she married Drew's dad, and they never saw any reason to move on. They treated the house and property like hallowed ground and had long been vocal about their wish that Drew, as their only child, would one day raise his family in this same house.

But Drew worked throughout college, saving money to set himself up upon graduation. Instead of taking a job in the city, he felt the world beckoning him out of the nest and went abroad. He traveled, partied, and met all sorts of interesting people. Along the way, he sometimes worked, earning where and when he could, and he'd gotten involved in several failed business ventures. All things considered, the money lasted longer than it probably should have. Even that wasn't enough to send him crawling back home. It was the nasty breakup with his Belgian girlfriend that left him disillusioned and lost. Literally lost. They were on some island in the Philippines when it happened. Drew didn't even know the name of the island.

In the shed, Drew finds a natty pair of gardening gloves, some shears, and a trowel. He digs around a bit more and discovers an old hand cultivator. With its three rusty, clawed tines, it looks like a horror movie prop.

It's not even noon and already sweltering. Sweat runs into his eyes, giving him a perpetual squint. He can hardly see a thing, but he can't wipe it out because his hands are filthy. The dirt is up to his elbows, and the sweat has turned it into a gooey, sticky, chalky mess.

As he squats beside the clump of weeds—still working on that first cluster, and there's half a dozen more spread around the yard—he's once again wondering what the hell he's doing here. He didn't really *need* to come home, but he had convinced himself it would be good for him. Just for a short while, of course. Long enough to get back on his feet. Find a job in the city, save a little money, introduce a sense of stability to his life. He never imagined his parents would treat him like some dopey kid fresh out of high school. Although, he should have expected it. Every time he spoke with his folks while he was away, never more than once a month, they would belittle his life choices, saying he belonged near home and ought to be cultivating a career, starting a family of his own. He'd put off those phone calls for weeks, sometimes months at a time.

When Drew pulls on the gloves, the scratches on his hands flare with pain. He winces, takes a few deep breaths, considers giving up. A real impetus to pack his bag and get the fuck out of dodge. But how? He doesn't have a vehicle and needs permission to take one of the cars. He'd have no choice but to hitchhike. Get as far away as he can. Out of state.

Would that be far enough? Could he find someone to carry him all the way to Mexico?

Instead, he uses the cultivator to dig around the weed, exposing a massive tangle of roots beneath the soil. Even with both hands pulling on the base of the stem, it will not come unearthed. Drew tries wedging the trowel underneath, but it won't penetrate. He has to dig out more dirt, eventually exposing a ball of roots twice the size of what he initially thought. Using the shears, he manages to snip off a few loose ends, but it barely makes a dent in the bulging mass.

More digging.

Now, Drew is squatting above the stubborn plant, straddling the two-foot wide hole he's dug up, bending at the knees with his gloved hands gripping the roots, poised like he's in a power-lifting competition.

A couple of deep breaths.

One. Two. Three—*Heave!*

Drew's entire body strains. His thighs burn. His lower back aches. He thrusts his hips.

The roots don't budge.

Then, something snaps. Drew is unexpectedly thrown backward. Fragments of dirt and roots fling into his face as his hands flail for something, anything to hold on to. He lands hard on his back, knocking the wind out of his lungs. He's stunned, dazed, gasping, and when he looks to the side, he sees that he has landed mere inches from the garden shears, which are open. The blades look menacingly sharp from this vantage, licking-distance from his eyeballs.

And his left eye is twitching. A bit of dirt must have landed there. Or a fleck of broken root. Or—*Oh Christ!*—a bug. It's itchy and starting to water. But he's got these gloves on, and even if he takes them off, his hands are too grimy. It'll only make it worse.

Breathing heavily, he rights himself and looks at his hands. Each fist is curled around a small bunch of roots that snapped off. The root-ball itself is unmoved, still lodged firmly in the ground.

"God*damnit!*"

"Watch your language around here, you lout." His mom comes trundling up from behind, glaring derisively, judging him, smirking. Is she...? Is she sneering? He can't tell because his left eye is so irritated that it won't open all the way, and sweat is trailing into his right eye. Everything's a blur.

"Ma! What am I doing here?"

"Good question."

"Don't you see this? There's no way I'm getting all these roots up. It's like a boulder."

"Did you really plan to come back after all this time and just loaf around? Think again, hotshot. You'd better get those weeds out today. Tomorrow you're cleaning out the gutters."

Drew rips off the gloves and throws them at one of the unplucked weeds. Through his bleary vision, it almost looks like the gloves bounce off, the stem remaining ramrod straight against the assault.

Inside the house, Drew locks himself in the bathroom. It takes five minutes to scrub his hands and arms, leaving a film of dirt in the sink. Finally, he can wipe the debris from his eye. Cool water to rinse it out. A wet rag to dab. Peeling back the lower lid, probing with a shaky finger, splashing more water, blinking furiously.

Nothing's there. Whatever got into his eye is gone now. Hopefully, he's flushed it out. His eye stays open, not all the way, but almost. Still itchy as hell, though.

Detouring into the kitchen, Drew peeks in the fridge, where he knows there are a few bottles of beer. He reaches in, thinking he'll chug one right there in the kitchen and bring another out into the sun to make his yardwork slightly more bearable.

But his hand pauses just before touching the bottles. He squeezes his eyes shut, glad at least for the cool blast of air, then clenches his fist and swears, his mom's voice already bleating in his ears.

The things she would say if she saw him with a beer before noon. She'd never let him hear the end of it.

Instead, he grabs the pitcher of filtered water.

Two hours later, Drew is still working at that very first batch of weeds when he makes an unsettling discovery.

Not only do the roots penetrate deeper into the soil than seems possible—no less than three feet, as far as he can tell, but maybe double that—they also appear to be connected to one another. The roots spread out like inverted mushroom clouds, linking to the roots of the weeds around them. Drew assumes they've become tangled, but he has yet to find any separation. If they are tangled, then it's worse than any ball of wires he's ever encountered. None of the roots seems to have an end, almost as though it's one linked system, all the weeds sprouting above the surface belonging to the same singular plant. Just this vast network of roots stretching out across... what? The entire property? Only the sheer implausibility allows Drew to put it out of his mind. That, and the continued discomfort in his left eye.

When his mom sees the crater he's hollowed out, she starts bawling at him. The last time anybody yelled at him like this was when Marianne finally left him in the Philippines. Stranded him, actually, because she knew he had hardly any money left. Listening to his mom's tirade, Drew has a flashback to that night by the beach. Marianne became so worked up that she lost her ability to speak English and slipped into vulgar Dutch. But it didn't matter. Drew didn't need a translator to decipher the anger and resentment and distrust and spite in her words. Then, the flashback transitions to childhood, Marianne morphing into his mother. How many times had he been playing in the yard and accidentally trampled her flowerbeds? Tracked mud into the house? Gotten carried away and returned after curfew?

The whole time his mom is screaming, Drew is trying to

get a word in. She won't listen. She doesn't care. She's standing right there, the hopelessly tangled roots literally at her feet, but she just refuses to see the problem. Drew's left eye twitches at her, and though she must notice, she ignores it.

"You think you're so smart, don't you? Look at you! Useless when it really matters! You've been out God-knows-where, wasting your life, letting opportunities slip by, just so you can, what? Claim yourself open-minded? Independent? Enlightened? That's real funny because all you are is a transient. No home, no job, no life. We offered you everything right here, built and cultivated just for you, *for your future!* But you only come crawling back when you've got nothing to offer and...*and you can't even help out when asked!* They're fucking weeds, Drew! Weeds! Just rip them out!"

He stopped listening a while ago. Even though he still can't open his left eye completely, he realizes it has stopped itching. A good sign. Maybe he'll be able to concentrate now, actually find a way to finish this bullshit job.

And when his mom storms off, saying she's going out and he "better be finished by the time she gets home," Drew breathes a sigh of relief. He pretends to pick at the roots until he hears her car drive off, then he shoves the hand cultivator into his back pocket and heads inside for those beers.

He brings three bottles back with him, chugging one as he walks.

The pit exposes the snarled mass of roots, stems sticking up like spines on the back of a prehistoric beast, the oddly colored leaves hanging limp and heavy. Another clump of these same weeds grows near the greenhouse, and a much larger group at the far end of the yard. Then there are the three near the house and the small batch out front. No way is he getting them all pulled up today.

The beer is cold and refreshing. As he pops the cap off the second bottle, he feels a sharp pinch on the left side of his temple, next to his eyebrow. It makes him flinch, and he wonders if he's been stung. A bee, a wasp—that's the last thing he needs. He places the chilled bottle against his cheekbone, slightly numbing the pain.

Drew walks around the dug-up earth and glares down at the tangled roots. He takes constant sips, quickly diminishing the contents of this second bottle. The punishing sun, the sweat, and the cold beer make him think of foreign beaches. Thailand, Australia, Peru. The Philippines...

Aaand there it is—Marianne. That night. The things they'd said, the names they'd called each other, all of it ruining what could have been a beautiful, lasting relationship. He doesn't want to think about her. He promised himself he wouldn't dwell on it. On her. On what could have, should have, would have been.

What would Marianne think if she saw him now? This pathetic return to home. Bossed around by Mommy and Daddy like a grunt. Hired help.

Jesus. That spot next to his eye really stings.

Drew finishes off the second bottle and drops it on the lawn. As he reaches for the third, he carefully touches the tender flesh in the soft spot right above his cheekbone.

"Oww, *fuck!*" he barks, pulling his hand away, squinting at the globule of blood on his fingertip.

Even more gently, using the fingernail this time, he touches the spot again. What feels like a tiny spine protrudes from his skin. The stinger of the pest that stung him, probably. It must have been huge to have left a stinger of that size, like the giant hornet that got into his dorm in Kyoto. Christ, that thing must have been two inches long. Head like a battering ram.

How could an insect like that have gotten near his face without him realizing it?

Drew opens the third beer, sipping this one rather than guzzling because, suddenly, he feels a bit ill. Since he can't see the spine without a mirror, he continues probing around on the side of his head, trying to visualize through touch. It sticks out maybe an eighth of an inch and is as sharp as a safety pin. It should be simple enough to extract, as long as it doesn't have anchors like a tick.

Pinching with his thumb and forefinger, Drew feels something else. On either side of the spine, it feels hard.

"The hell is that...?"

Pressing down produces an unfamiliar pressure. The same spot on the right side of his face is soft and pliable, as usual. The tough skin around the spine is definitely not normal, but nothing to be too concerned about. It can't be. Just some severe swelling from the sting of whatever monstrous insect snuck up on him.

"*Ahhhh!*"

Something wrenches painfully on Drew's left eye. The eyelid clamps shut, pinched from the inside. He feels his eyeball being squashed and pulled inward.

The bottle falls from his hand. Drew bats uselessly at his face, falls to his knees, writhing and moaning in agony.

It must be coming from the spine. Some kind of venom? He recalls stories about the funnel-web spider in Australia, the debilitating pain, the sweating and vomiting, the cutting off of the airways. Death. But there are no critters like that here; only garden snakes, wasps, and daddy longlegs.

When he calms down, he tentatively, gently, touches the spine again.

Impossible.

It's longer. A lot longer. It must be sticking out almost half an inch now. And it's not like his body is rejecting it or pushing it out. It feels thicker, too, like it's growing and embedded firmly at the base. He can actually grab it between the tips of his fingers, but it won't move. A tiny steel post driven into his head. There's a movie character like that. Those *Hellraiser* films. Some kind of sexually deviant demon who tortures his victims for pain and pleasure.

Drew finds no pleasure in this. He still can't open his left eye. This fucking spine needs to come out.

His hand quivers as he feels around his temple. Is it even longer now? Still growing? Three-quarters of an inch? With it squeezed tightly between his right thumb and forefinger, Drew clenches his jaw, takes a deep breath, and grunts in advance, steeling himself as he yanks it out.

A lightning flash of pain explodes on the side of his face. The spine resists, then gives way, coming free with relative ease. But that tearing sound can't be good. Drew doesn't even scream. The shock and unwillingness to believe have stolen his voice. His right eye bulges with worry. He's afraid to move his fingers, still clamped around the spine.

And it burns like crazy—not just the spot where the spine was, but the whole area beside his eye.

He wants a closer look at the spine, but it won't move. He can only pull it a few centimeters before inducing a searing pain.

Jesus Christ—it's still attached.

Drew lets go, but nothing falls. A flap of flesh droops limply above his cheekbone, with a small patch of exposed dermis stinging wildly in the fresh air. A drop of sweat trickles into it, bringing a shock of pain as Drew stands and races toward the house.

At the bathroom mirror, Drew sees the grotesque and incomprehensible sight of removed flesh and begins to hyperventilate. A patch of skin the size of a quarter has simply torn away from his face. It hangs from the corner of his eye, just below the eyebrow. The spine pokes through the center, but it is no mere stinger. Underneath the flesh-flap, it's connected to a wiry network of filaments that stretches outward like a spiderweb buried beneath the epidermis.

There's no way to tell how far it has spread. His left eye is still pinched shut, feeling like it's been stapled from the inside.

Drew can't think straight. What the hell is he to do? He's the only one at home. His parents have the cars. He could dial 911, but what does he tell them? This doesn't even make sense. He might be tripping, hallucinating, or losing his mind, but there's no way this is real. And even if it is, it can't be as bad as it looks. It'll be some creepy crawly parasite he picked up from a tainted water supply in the backwoods of Guatemala or wherever. He'll need to visit a hospital to be patched up and get a prescription for an antiparasitic. No big deal. But, for now, he has to get a grip on himself and remove this invader from his body.

When he touches it, his hand recoils. Instead of slimy and squiggly like he expects, it feels oddly dry and firm. Drew leans closer to the mirror, trying to get a better look with his one good eye.

It's fibrous.

Like the stem of a plant.

"The hell...?"

It looks just like those goddamn roots.

Drew staggers to the window, pushes the curtains aside, and stares into the backyard. He's shaking his head. Uh-uh. No way. Not possible. Even if some tiny shrapnel of the roots landed in his eye, it could not possibly have grown and spread this fast.

As if in response, the pinching behind his left eye intensifies. Something is crushing his eyeball, dragging it deeper into his skull.

Back to the mirror, Drew hangs over the sink, making sure he's got a firm grip on the tangled mess of vine-like strands.

And he yanks it, screeching in anguish as it lifts and tears away. The bathroom's silence allows him to hear his flesh separating, peeling back like duct tape off its roll. The thin filaments stretch over his orbital bones onto his forehead, and the skin is lifted clear away up to his scalp.

In a panic, he pulls harder, an incredulous voice in his head screaming that it cannot possibly have spread any further, that it has to pop loose soon, like a cork.

With each tug, his facial flesh rips a little more. It shouldn't be this easy. The human body is robust and resilient.

Isn't it?

It hurts so much that Drew's screams have transitioned to panting. One wild eye bulges aimlessly from its socket, tracking the absurd sight of his flesh freed from the constraints of his face, the illogical net of interlocked vines or legs or roots or whateverthefuck. It keeps going, apparently spread all over his face, just below the surface. Some sort of super-fungus? He's not sure he even wants to know; he just wants it out of his body. Now that he's seen how widespread it is, he can't shake the revolting feeling that it's still spreading, reaching down his extremities, twining with his rib cage, soon to infiltrate his organs.

Drew's entire forehead has been torn away. It hangs down from the eyebrows, covering his view of the mirror, which, in a way, seems like a grace. He doesn't have to look at the horrid sight of himself as he continues pulling, in the other direction now, down his jawbone. The vicious sound of tearing flesh jolts him back from a daze. At the bottom of his chin, it becomes harder to pull. It's stuck.

Maybe this is the end. All it took was the disfigurement of half his face. He lifts the flap of skin away from his good eye. The entire left side of his face is literally fleshless. The sight reminds him of that girl he saw in Laos; she'd been out in the fields sweeping for mines near Phonsavan when one triggered and mutilated her once attractive features.

But he's so close to being rid of this disgusting, painful, invasive thing—*Why won't it come loose?*

Desperation overflows from Drew, spewing from his mouth in a wordless plea for help. His legs give out and he crumples to the floor. Something stabs into his ass, shooting him back to his feet.

No no no no!

It couldn't have reached that far down his body... could it?

He feels around and scratches his hand on something at

his belt line. Have they poked right out of his ass cheek and penetrated his jeans?

No. It's just the hand cultivator. Three long, sharp prongs, bent like a claw, shaped for quickly tearing into dirt, grinding it down to fine grains.

And raking out stubborn weeds.

Drew removes the cultivator and looks at it. As he lifts up the flap of forehead skin, the impossible knot of twined fibers scratches his fingertips.

And he knows what he has to do.

Ten minutes later, the front door bursts open. Heavy footsteps tread along the hardwood floors. His mom's voice sounds at once distant and clearer than ever before.

"Drew! Drew? Where are you?"

He hears her moving through the house, imagines her glancing into each room, peeking out the window into the backyard where he should still be de-weeding.

"Drew, sweetie, I feel just awful about what I said before. I didn't mean it. Your father and I really are glad to have you home. You're welcome as long as you want. We're proud of you. We are. But we hope you'll stick around, find a job in the city, and remain close as we approach retirement. Drew?"

His entire body throbs and burns. His voice is shot. Nothing more than a weak, wet croak emerges from his throat. The floor trembles as his mom moves down the hall. Getting closer, closer, her voice louder, more insistent.

"We just think it's time for you to put down some roots. Start a family of your own. We have no intention of selling the house. Maybe a few acres. But it will all be yours. And it would be such a waste if you didn't have anyone to share it with..."

And he can't stop. It's already gone too far, but he must be close. Maybe just one more strong scrape and it will all come loose. Fall away like a hospital gown.

"Drew? Where are you? In the bathroom?"

He answers with a hollow whine that echoes eerily off the tile and porcelain.

"I hope you're presentable because I'm not alone. You'll never guess who I ran into at the supermarket. You remember Louise Palmero, don't you? Her family used to live just up the road from here when you two were in school. Same grade, I believe. Isn't that right, Louise?"

A mumbled, inaudible reply from the hall.

A sloppy, gagging cough from Drew.

"She's grown into a lovely young woman, Drew. Why don't you come out and say hello? Maybe you can take the car into town and have a nice dinner together. Catch up and, well... who knows? Drew? Drew? What are you doing in there?"

In the silent pause, all that can be heard is a repulsive tearing sound, like bark being removed from a waterlogged tree trunk.

"Drew? Honey? What was that? The door's open, so I'm going to—"

The hand cultivator clatters into the sink. Drew looks up at the mirror. Muscle tissue, tendons, and bones stare back at him. His nose has been reduced to a small lump of cartilage. Droplets of blood on his hairless scalp reflect the light above. A curtain of red trails down his neck and shoulders. Exposed veins pulse and leak on his throat, chest, and arms. Wounds spew blood where the cultivator dug in too deep.

Behind his own gory, mutilated features, the door swings open. He emits a wretched moan that means *I give up*, but the two women standing in the doorway have no clue what he's trying to convey. Their shocked screams penetrate like lances. They don't move, but only stare at the gruesome, bloodied pulp standing before them, then raise their hands to cover their eyes.

Drew drops his skin, still bound to the strange root-like mesh underneath. It hangs from his waist, a grisly natural skirt. Flashes of pain attack him all over the exposed tissue, which now makes up most of his upper body and head. Grouped in threes, deep grooves run along his tender muscles, leaking blood in steady streams. Those womanly howls of terror rattle his brain, making him dizzy, nauseous, almost disembodied. Blood has soiled the floor mat below, sprayed across the mirror, and pooled on the countertop.

Drew reaches into the sink for the cultivator. Maybe they can help him.

They can remove these invasive roots from his body.

He turns back to face them, holding it out, offering them this tool that has gotten him so far already.

But Louise runs screaming from the house, the front door slamming behind her. And his mom has fallen to the ground in a dead faint.

Bearded Vulture

I

The ledge ends in a sheer drop. Hundreds of feet below, ocean waves crash against the rocky shore. He's going to jump. He doesn't want to, but he's going to. He has to. This is the way it ends.

No. No, he can't. He won't. It's too high. He's not ready for the end. He'll never be ready for *this* end.

As he tries to step away, someone or something shoves him from behind. The blow sends him flailing over the ledge, tumbling, plummeting toward the black sea as he lets out a shrill cry—

Gil wakes with a gasp. The piercing wail lingers, fading gradually, but he doesn't shoot out of bed or look around or check his phone. He knows that scream. It's been years since he last heard it, but having the dream again brings it all back.

Everything he hated about his former life rises, swirls, and foams within him, just like those waves far below.

He has finally escaped that powder keg of a life. Cut ties with his fraudulent family and ventured out on his own. Started afresh. A new life in a new town without the burden of his parents' secrets to weigh him down.

Gil looks to his left at the spray of long blonde hair fanned out beside him. Her breathing comes with a steady, adorable wheeze. At first, Gil thinks the soothing sound will ease him back to sleep. But the dream has stirred something within. Or maybe it was the sex. He can't quite tell. Both were thrilling in different ways. They each sparked a flame that he feared might never burn again.

Lauren is unlike any woman he has known. She is willful, curious, and independent. He never expected her to come back to his apartment, let alone stay the night. And he never imagined he would connect with someone after only a week in this new life, all alone in this small Adirondack town.

For the first time since he came east, he feels that he made the right choice. He had to get away, had to start over, and even though the town of Pickett's Post was an arbitrary decision, Lauren has helped him start to see that everything will be okay. And she has done it over the course of a single night. For the first time in as long as Gil can remember, he is eager to get on with his life and hopeful for what's to come.

The preserved foot sits on the desk where Lauren left it. As Gil struggles to fall back to sleep, he stares at its angular shape perched in the darkness and thinks again that he should have left it behind. He hasn't brought much other than clothes, but during a hurried, last-minute packing session, he grabbed a few items with no connection to his family. The hope was that they'd give him a head start, a way to reframe himself as the person he was always supposed to be.

Then again, maybe the only way to start over is to toss every last part of himself over that ledge, watching as it smashes on the rocks below and the black sea washes it all away.

2

GIL STANDS BEFORE THE TRAILHEAD, map in hand, asking himself if this is really how he wants to spend the afternoon. It's not too late to head home. But then, what's he going to do with the rest of his day? He should be out trying to secure a job for the approaching summer tourist season, though there's a voice in his head that sounds conspicuously like a gross amalgamation of his folks, and it's prodding his inherited laziness.

Why would a rich kid like you bus tables or serve appetizers to the upper class?

He checks the map again, confirming for the fourth time that this is the right trail. It has to be. According to the map, it's the only one.

"Don't go in there."

The tiny voice comes from behind. Gil spins around, searching for the speaker. A little girl lurks nearby, eyeing him with a look that might be either warning or contempt.

Gil hitches the backpack on his shoulders and grins at the girl. "Why not?"

"It's haunted, that's why."

"Maybe that's why I wanna go in there," Gil says, playfully raising an eyebrow.

Wild laughter erupts nearby. Both Gil and the girl jump as a middle-aged couple emerges from the trail. The woman howls with laughter while her husband hunches forward, clutching his gut.

Gil kinks his head at the couple. "*They* don't seem too scared."

"It's true," insists the girl. "Ghosts and monsters. They're real..."

"Have you seen them?"

The girl sneers at Gil and takes a step closer. She's on the verge of speaking her mind when two adolescent boys come charging out of the trail, screaming their lungs out. Their screams are laced with terror, but their expressions are excited and gleeful. They run right between Gil and the girl, who jumps back to avoid being plowed over by the older boys. The boys catch up to their still-laughing parents. When Gil turns back to the girl, she's scowling at him.

"There's a—" she starts, but is cut off by a man running over.

"Sheila, honey? What are you doing? Leave him alone, will you?" The girl's father glances at Gil and rests a hand on his daughter's shoulder. "Go back and help your mother, okay?"

The girl glances at the trailhead. A shriek rings out high above. They all look up at the hawk circling overhead. When Gil glances down, the girl is staring at him again. Something flashes behind her eyes, and then, without another word, she takes off toward her mother at one of the picnic tables. The father watches her go, then steps toward Gil.

"Sorry about that..." he says, embarrassed.

Gil smiles. "Don't worry about it."

"Don't listen to her. These trails," the man points at the trailhead, "they're fine. They're, you know...they're quite nice. Not too difficult."

Gil nods, waiting for more, but the man just stares at him with a strained smile. "Good to know," Gil says and starts to walk away. "Thanks."

The man jumps forward as though to block Gil's path. He hesitates, glancing back at his family, then steps closer and points to the left. "It's that one."

"Sorry?"

"The haunted mountain. It's that one. No trails over there, though. So, uh...you shouldn't have to worry about accidentally wandering onto it. Stick to the trails and you'll be fine."

"Ah, yeah..." Gil smiles and nods, holding up the hand-drawn map. The man peers at it and notices the lipstick kiss. Backing away, he squints at Gil with a contemptuous look that proves he is the girl's father.

Gil raises a hand for an awkward farewell and walks onto the trailhead.

3

THE TRAIL STARTS at a steep incline, and it's wide, leaving plenty of room for hikers to pass each other. According to Lauren's map, drawn from memory, several branching trails wind up the mountain's slopes, all linking to this one trailhead. He'll have to hike just about to the top to reach the pass leading to the sister mountain—Mount Tomb, as the locals refer to it. All officially maintained trails are on this mountain, with the more welcoming name of Sunrise Hill, but Lauren said the old trails on Mount Tomb should still be navigable.

The forest is not very dense. Looking ahead, Gil can see the colorful shirts of other hikers. Most of them are hiking down. Gil meant to leave his apartment earlier, but he'd stayed up so late with Lauren and expended so much energy that he wound up falling asleep on the sofa after lunch.

Birds flutter and sing all around him. The leaves are a brilliant spring green, and the forest is still damp from a dawn shower. Patches of wildflowers grow alongside the trail. Sharply defined rays of sunlight pierce the canopy, lighting the trail and trees with effervescent splashes of color.

Gil walks at an easy pace, absorbing the sights, smells, and sounds, and his mind wanders back to the night before.

"That's not possible!" Lauren squealed with shock. "How can someone live on the coast all their life and never once eat sushi? That settles it. Change of plans. I don't feel like Italian anyway."

"I won't eat it," Gil persisted.

"Don't you want to know what it's like?"

"Not even a bit."

"Oh, come on! Try it before you bash it!" Lauren laughed.

"Cooked seafood is one thing. No problem. Grilled is even better. But you come at me with the raw stuff, and I'm going the other way."

"What-oh-what are we going to do, then? I've already changed our plans. I'm taking you to the best sushi place in the Adirondacks. Looks like you'll have to put on your big boy pants, Gil Rilke."

"Then our date comes to an early, anticlimactic end. Unless you want to meet up again after solo dinners."

Lauren considered this for a moment before breaking into a bright smile. She grabbed his hand and led him across the street. "Fine. We'll compromise. We also happen to have the best grilled seafood you'll find Upstate."

"Why are there so many seafood options way up here in the mountains?"

"To feed all the rich assholes from Manhattan who own property up here. Fortunately, it's still too early in the season for them. None of the restaurants have jacked up their prices yet."

Coming to a break in the trail, Gil stops to consult the map. A group of three teenagers approaches from behind. They head to the right, not even stopping to consider the fork. Gil's map directs him to the left. The teens whisper as they sneak peeks at Gil going the other way.

The restaurant was in a part of town Gil hadn't explored yet. After dinner and a few drinks, Lauren walked him home, partly to show him the way, but also because they'd been having a lively conversation that neither wanted to end. As they walked, they traded stories about their childhoods. Gil spoke of his youth as honestly as he could, explaining why he left without giving too many details. Lauren had been in Boston for school the past few years and only recently returned. Her stories of growing up in Pickett's Post captivated Gil. He didn't even realize they'd turned onto his block and were standing out front of his apartment building.

"This is your place, isn't it?" Lauren asked.

"What? Oh, yeah. How did you know?"

"Growing up in a place like this, you tend to know every nook and cranny."

"Do you approve?" Gil asked, kinking his head at the old brick building.

"Mmm... I'd have to see the inside to make a fair assessment."

"Thanks for walking me. I might have wandered all night before finding my way back here. Really need to familiarize myself with these streets."

Lauren smiled. "And thank you for dinner."

"You took me there. I should—"

"It was fun, is what I meant. You know...this was my first good experience with the app. I used it at school and met a lot of real dirtbags."

"First time for me. So, one hundred percent success, I guess. I was hesitant to try it, but...I'm glad I did."

"You know, it's not that late. If you want me to judge your living situation, you could invite me up..."

"Yeah, of course..."

As soon as Gil shut the door behind them, they were drawn together. Lauren didn't get so much as a single glance at the apartment. They were all over each other before Gil could even turn on a light.

Gil stops to rest at the top of a steep flight of wooden stairs inlaid on the trail. He takes the water bottle from his backpack and drinks half of it. He's been too lost in thought to know how long he's been climbing. He moves to the side as a man rounds the corner ahead and blows past, descending the stairs. Three more men follow, each separated by thirty or forty paces. None of them are talking, so Gil can't tell whether they're together or hiking solo.

Breathing heavily, Gil continues upward. He assumes—and hopes—that he is approaching the pass that leads to Mount Tomb.

The sex was the best Gil had ever had. They'd both drunk three cocktails and a couple of shots after dinner, which did away with any inhibitions. Gil guessed that Lauren probably didn't have many inhibitions to begin with, but he sure did.

They lay in the dark for a while, splayed across the bed, pillow talk and wandering hands. Eventually, Lauren got chilly and slipped under the covers. Gil joined her and finally switched on the bedside lamp, allowing Lauren to see her surroundings for the first time.

"When did you say you moved in?" she asked, astounded.

"Last Friday."

"A week already? You've hardly unpacked a thing."

"I've been kinda...unpacking my mind all week. I wasn't too sure about this move. Leaving everything, everyone. Settling in a place like this. Not knowing any—"

Lauren abruptly sat up, startling Gil. He stared at her breasts while she pointed at a pair of boxes in the corner.

"What the hell is *that?*"

"What?"

"That!"

Pulling his eyes away from her body, Gil saw what she was pointing at. It sat on the floor between the boxes.

"Oh, that's a... It's a preserved foot."

She gaped at him, waiting for an explanation. When he offered none, she jumped out of bed and grabbed one of his shirts from a pile of clothes before skittering back to the bed with the foot.

Mounted on a heavy wooden base and held erect by a thin

iron bar, the leg stood more than twelve inches tall. With the talons, the toes were as large as Lauren's outstretched hand.

Stupefied, at a loss for words, her eyes bugging out of her head, Lauren could barely give voice to her thoughts. "I mean...but...why?"

"I got it in Athens. The guy told me it was the foot of a Siren."

"A Siren? Like...the mythical singing women?"

Gil shrugged and sat up against the headboard, pulling the comforter to cover himself. "I was eight. This street peddler had it on display with his t-shirts and keychains. He saw me staring at it and fed me this story about how Sirens still lived on the remote Aegean island where he was from. He said they would cast themselves off the seaside cliffs when it was time for them to die and that they sometimes washed up in his village."

Lauren smirked and got up to look around the room. The heavy base thudded when she set it on Gil's desk.

She peeked into a box and asked, "Do you mind?"

"Unpack it all if you want to." As she scanned a few book covers, Gil stared at her bare ass and felt the stirrings of another erection. Averting his gaze back to the foot, he continued. "I showed it to my high school biology teacher once. She thought it probably came from a bearded vulture. Still pretty rare..."

The vintage set of tarot cards momentarily held Lauren's attention. Less so, the bust of Edgar Allen Poe. She shuddered when she took out the framed antique photos of ghosts and carnival sideshow freaks, and the hand-painted Ouija board made her cringe. She quickly set it aside and found a few more books.

"I remember these..." She held up the three slim volumes with their creepy cover illustrations—*Scary Stories to Tell in the Dark.*

"My favorite books as a kid," Gil said.

"I hated them. You've got a lot of bizarre shit."

"When I was leaving, those were the only things that didn't remind me of my parents. Of *what* I was leaving. Everything else came from a life I didn't choose and never wanted anything to do with. The things in that box represent a side of me that I curated myself. That stuff, it's not really me anymore, but...I guess I wanted something to remind me who I am. Or help me figure it out. It sounds stupid..."

"No, it doesn't. I think it's great, what you're doing. Starting over like this. It doesn't matter why you left or why you chose such an isolated place as Pickett's Post. You can tell me someday if you want to. Whatever the reasons, it shows courage. I couldn't do it. After graduating, I got job offers all over the country, but here I am, right back in the same backwoods town I tried so hard to leave behind."

Lauren brought one of the books back to the bed. She stretched out beside Gil, flipping through the pages and shivering in disgust at the images inside.

"So, young Gil Rilke was a bit of a closeted weirdo. There must be a trace of it left, otherwise you wouldn't have kept this stuff. So, what is it? I suppose you're into true crime documentaries and serial killer podcasts and all that."

"Those kinds of stories creep me out. Real-life boogeymen were always a bit too much for me. But..." He trailed off and turned away.

"But what?"

"I still watch ghost hunter shows sometimes. Haunted

houses. Creature sightings. It's the paranormal that always interested me."

"Ugh!" Lauren slapped his bare chest playfully. "I should have known! With your dragon's foot or whatever it is!" She began to tickle him. He resisted until she threw her leg over his waist, pinning him down.

When she finally stopped, they both had to catch their breath from laughter.

"Well, since you're such a freak for the strange and mysterious, I guess you'll want to check out our haunted mountain."

Gil adjusted himself beneath her, his fingers digging into her hips ever so slightly.

"Haunted mountain?"

4

ANOTHER SET of inlaid stairs brings Gil to the top of a steep rise. It's not the summit, but the peak of Sunrise Hill is visible from where he stands. He considers resting for a few minutes, but the angle of the sunlight tells him daylight is waning. The hike has taken longer than he thought, and he hasn't even reached the haunted mountain yet. Any delay might mean he's hiking down in the dark.

Here, the trail branches off in several directions. A sign posted beside a crude bench indicates that the trail on the right leads to the peak, the trail straight ahead circles the peak, and the path on the left descends down the slope, eventually connecting back to the main trail. Another, less conspicuous path is unmarked and overgrown. If someone wasn't looking for it, they would miss it.

Though the details of Lauren's map aren't clear, this must be the trail that leads to the pass.

"We used to go up there sometimes in high school," Lauren had explained. "That's the sort of thing kids do around here during their rebellious phase. Like a rite of passage. They go there to hide out, get drunk, get high. Couples go to make out or get laid. Some even try and search for the...uh, for thrills, I guess."

Noting her hesitation, Gil pressed for more. "Search for what?"

"The, uh... Shit. I shouldn't have brought it up."

"What?"

"The bodies."

It's been a while since Gil saw any other hikers, so he tenses up when he hears footsteps crunching through fallen leaves. He looks around, unsure of which direction they're coming from.

A man and woman appear ahead on the trail that wraps around the peak. The woman glances at Gil as she passes.

"Hi," she smiles.

"Hello," answers Gil. He considers asking them about the unmarked trail, just to be sure. But when he notices the man scrutinizing his indecision, he abruptly pushes through the overhanging branches.

Behind him, Gil hears the man mutter under his breath.

"Hey, buddy, you sure you wanna go in there?"

The woman hisses playfully and slaps the man's arm. "Cut it out!"

They fail to stifle their laughter as they descend the stairs.

Though the trail is narrower than the main trails, it doesn't seem unused, forgotten, or forbidden. There is still a clear walking path. Some of the trees are marked with initials and hearts. It's on a slight decline, which allows Gil to pick up his pace.

"What bodies?" he'd asked.

Lauren pulled the covers up to her chin and looked away. She sighed and said, "It happened a long time ago. Before I was born. This guy—the newspapers called him Pickett's Curse—he would mutilate his victims in town but take their bodies with him. Even though he never cleaned up the crime scenes, they never found evidence to identify him. Then, one day, after ten years or something, he just turned himself in. There was no DNA or fingerprints or murder weapons, but he confessed and said he'd taken all the bodies up on that mountain. Said they were still up there, but he refused to say where. They locked him up based on his confession alone. Never found a trace of the bodies, though."

"What was his name?"

"I don't know. It sounded close to *hell*, I think. People used to say that 'the victims got on Hell's bad side.' It might have been Hall or something like that."

"How many did he kill?"

With a shiver, Lauren said, "Nine? Ten? I think he only killed about once a year. I never knew all the details. It's just, you know...the kind of story kids overhear and tell to scare each other shitless." She gazed at Gil and shrugged, clearly apprehensive to be speaking of such things. "It scares adults, too. That's why no one goes up there. I'm sure high schoolers still go to fuck and get stoned and prove their worth or whatever, but nobody else does."

"You have to take me."

"Uh-uh. I won't. Not for anything. I would like to see you again, but I'll just show you around town, thank you very much."

"Why? Did you see something up there?"

"No. I never saw anything. But...it's more like a feeling. The air or something. It always felt colder, darker. It gets inside you. Makes you feel that everything is wrong. Or black. Or rotten."

"I understand," Gil said. He rubbed Lauren's back. "So, where is it?"

"It was a joke, Gil. You don't want to go up there."

"All the stuff you pulled out of that box, that was the only part of me that I recognized as *me*. I'm not saying that thoughts of ghosts keep me up at night anymore, but... As a kid, I was obsessed with the paranormal. I've never witnessed anything myself or even felt anything like what you just described."

"Then how can you believe in it?"

"Who said I do? More like I *wanted* to believe. I wished it was real."

"But you were just a kid."

"Moving here, starting over like this...it's sort of like being a kid again, isn't it? This might be a good opportunity to, I don't know...figure out who I really am."

The trail suddenly opens up. Most of the trees and understory are dead or dying. Ahead on the left is a large wooden platform, an outlook overlooking the park below and the town beyond. Once, it might have offered a sweeping panorama, but now heavy, drooping boughs obscure the view.

The planks creak and bend, the wood weatherworn and

termite-eaten. Several posts in the railing have fallen out. The whole platform tilts slightly to the right. It must be fifty years old.

Cautiously, Gil approaches the railing and peers through the branches. He's higher than he thought. The people in the park are the size of ants, and there are fewer than when he arrived. The fact that they're heading home is an indication that Gil better not linger.

A loud fluttering startles him. The entire platform lurches and sways as an enormous crow perches on the railing. It watches Gil, then hops along the rail, inching closer. Each time the bird hops, the platform rocks and groans. Gil imagines the old, rotted wood giving way, sending him tumbling down a drop of maybe twenty-five feet, enough to break a few bones and make the hike down inconceivable. The crow knocks its beak on the railing a few times and stares at Gil. Its beak opens wide, releasing no sound at first. Then, a low clicking emits from its throat. The clicking continues as the crow hops closer, one eye on Gil the entire time. With one more glance down at the park, Gil carefully back-steps onto the trail and moves along.

Still thinking about the rickety platform and the nosy bird, Gil does not hear the old woman approaching. As he's glancing back at the crow, which is still watching him, he nearly walks smack into her. She appears to be in her late sixties or early seventies. Without offering a word, she glowers at Gil as she passes, lurching with a painful hobble. A loaded canvas bag weighs her down. Gil wants to ask if she's lost or needs help, but she doesn't look like the chatty type. Gil cannot comprehend how someone of that age got all the way up the mountain on her own. And she came from the direction of the haunted mountain. If not for her hateful glare, he might have stopped her to ask what she was doing over there, whether the stories are true, and how she manages to keep her aged bones in good enough shape for such strenuous climbing. Instead, he only stares, listening to the sound of wood clinking in her bag until she's no longer visible through the branches.

That morning, after Gil utilized the full extent of his cooking skills to make breakfast—coffee, toast, and scrambled eggs—Lauren finally gave in. She drew the map on the back of a DIY instruction manual. From Gil's apartment, getting to the park was a straight shot, a pleasant thirty-minute walk through town. The park spread out beneath the sister mountains to the north. Though Lauren claimed to have little memory of the trails, she traced them without ever second-guessing herself.

"I understand your curiosity," she said as she jotted a few finishing touches, indicating important junctions. "But seriously, just stick to Sunrise Hill. You'll get close enough to Mount Tomb. You'll feel the change in the air, I swear. No need to risk getting lost on those mangy, overgrown trails."

"Mount Tomb?"

"You know? Like Mount Doom from—"

"Yeah, I know," Gil smiled.

"Clever, huh? That's what people have called it since...I don't know when. But it's not just because of the mountain's history. It really is dangerous. The town has a crew that clears all the local trails except on Mount Tomb. It's not forbidden or illegal, but there are real risks. A lot of steep drops, no guard rails. And there's no telling how the ground will hold up on those ridges."

"I'll be careful. I just need to get out. Something like this will distract me, maybe help to settle my mind. I'm starting to like it here. I should learn about the town's dark past. And if I happen to see a ghost or two along the way, all the better."

Lauren snorted and reached for her compact mirror. She checked her makeup and then finished her coffee. "Alright," she sighed. "Usually, I like stubborn people. But this time... I guess it's my fault. I shouldn't have enticed you with that story in the first place. You never would have known. So, now I'll get to see just how brave Gil Rilke really is. Pretty soon you'll be scarfing raw fish, raw beef, and God knows what else."

"Barf," said Gil.

"Just don't call on me to come and rescue you." Lauren touched up her lipstick and stared at Gil earnestly. "I won't do it."

"How about afterward?"

"A second date already? Eager little adventurer, aren't you? I'll be with a friend all afternoon, and I'm supposed to have dinner with my parents, but... Maybe later tonight. I'll get back to you."

With that, Lauren picked up the map. She shook her head and glared at it before bringing it to her lips and planting a perfect lipstick kiss over the words *Mount Tomb*. Then, she stood up and shoved the map at Gil, letting go before he even took it.

Lying on the ground beside the trail is an old, dented stop sign. The yellowed lettering melts into a backdrop the color of bloody vomit. Beneath the word STOP, someone has scrawled a warning in a childish script—

Go back! Bodies never laid to rest,
left to wander, lead the living to death...

A great conversation piece for his new living room if he could lug it down the mountain. It's not very heavy, but it's unwieldy and too large to fit in his backpack. A few of the bent edges are sharp, so he would need to be extremely careful and surefooted. For now, he leaves it lying in the weeds.

Ahead, the trail splits in two. One path can hardly be called a trail at all, and the other is the pass to the next mountain. Lauren cautioned him repeatedly about the pass, telling him it had always been narrow. But this is even thinner than he expected. Heavy rains appear to have chipped away at the northern ridge, leaving a steep drop and less than a foot of walking room. Just looking at it makes Gil dizzy. For the first time, he considers turning back. If he could get the stop sign down, he would at least have a souvenir for his troubles.

But taking the sign without actually visiting the haunted mountain would be dishonest. A lie. A fraud. Just like his parents, taking all that money from gullible folks year after year, living like royalty without lifting a finger, without ever fulfilling all their grand promises and guarantees, and unrepentant while their victims wallowed in poverty.

He can't do it. He won't. That is precisely why he left, why he came here to Pickett's Post, the middle of nowhere at the other end of the country. No one knows where he is. He didn't tell anyone he was leaving. He'd spent a few days preparing in secret and then simply disappeared, leaving no way for anyone to track him down. He's already made the deep dive into this new life, so the least he can do is strive to live honestly.

Gil picks up the stop sign and leans it against a tree trunk in front of the pass, positioning it just so. His phone has a full battery, but it's getting poor reception. It keeps switching between one and two bars. The time is already 4:54. He needs to keep moving, but first, he steps back to take a picture of the pass with the graffitied stop sign in the lower right corner. He sends the photo to Lauren with a message.

"Found the pass."

He pockets his phone and starts off. With his first step onto the narrow walkway, he pauses and takes a deep breath. Halfway across, he hears his phone *ding*. The sound startles him, throwing him off balance and forcing him to look down. From this angle, the drop looks even steeper and more treacherous. His heart pounds, and before he can consider what he's doing, he's racing the rest of the way across.

Running without thinking makes it easier. Before he knows it, he's breathing heavily on Mount Tomb's eastern slope.

Still catching his breath, Gil takes out his phone, opens Lauren's reply.

"Don't do it, Gil."

"Too late," Gil responds. *"This lipstick kiss has seduced me..."*

"Nice line, you creep, but it's a bad idea."

"Can't help it, irresistible... Meet later?"

He sends the message and gazes ahead while he waits for a response. The tree cover is considerably thicker than on Sunrise Hill. The canopy is dense, letting in very little light. He hears birds fluttering through branches, but gone are chirps and birdsong. It is eerily quiet. Glancing back at the narrow pass, he dreads having to cross over it again. To ensure he has light to return by, he can't stand here waiting forever.

With one more look at his phone, he pockets it and starts onto Mount Tomb.

5

AFTER A WHILE, the trail is essentially non-existent. Branches hang into the path at every step. Gil's arms have been scratched to hell from brushing them out of the way. Bushes and weeds spill from both sides onto the six-inch footpath. He barely has room to set his feet without snagging them on some growth, slowing his pace to a crawl.

Gil hopes the low light is a result of the dense forest, but he starts to worry that time has gotten away from him. He's been trudging the slope on what feels like a wandering route, and he's no longer replaying his evening with Lauren, too preoccupied by the trail's difficulty. Other than the treacherous drop along the pass, he hasn't seen anything worrisome. But Lauren was right about how it feels. There's a heaviness to the air that differs from Sunrise Hill. A prickliness that makes Gil's skin tingle and alerts him to the utter stillness. There is almost no breeze, no rustling of leaves or swaying of stalks. He hears no more birds calling or fluttering through the branches, and no hikers are tromping up ahead, laughing and chatting as they make their way. Sure, those things are easily explained, but like any good campfire story, a nagging doubt remains. A suspicion that all logical explanations are only a kind of smokescreen for the ghoulish truth.

It has grown so dim that Gil has trouble following the

thinning trail. He pauses, glancing back, and is disconcerted to see that the path is no more visible behind than ahead. Briefly, his mind battles his perception—the traveled road must be easier to recognize than the untrodden path to come.

The sensible thing would be to forfeit now while there's still enough light to get down.

But he's already here. He's made it this far. He never really believed he would see a ghost or witness some unexplainable, supernatural phenomenon. That's not what this is about. It's supposed to be about finding himself. And it has been a pleasant afternoon. A lovely day of hiking. He has had plenty of time to think and mostly just wishes for more time with Lauren. He could turn around now and meet her this evening, telling her how he traversed the slopes and summited the haunted mountain, conquering the past and freeing the obsessive little boy trapped inside him. He could, but to do so would be to stoop to his parents' level, scheming and twisting words to get what they wanted from unsuspecting folks. Or, he could turn back now and tell Lauren the truth—that he made it to Mount Tomb and felt those eerie hallmarks of all haunted places. Gooseflesh. Jitters. Sounds without sources and passing shadows without bodies.

But if he goes just a little further, maybe he can probe these unsettling sensations and come away better for it. Maybe he can satisfy all his curiosities *and* emerge as the strong, honest man he wants to be.

He pushes onward. At once, a spiny branch snags his T-shirt, tearing the sleeve. Pausing to detach the twig, he jumps when a bird calls loudly up ahead. As soon as he's free, he takes off again, ducking under another branch. He slips his phone out of his pocket.

"Shit…"

It's already 5:48. Still a couple of hours until sunset, but he can hardly see a thing the way it is. Gil glances behind him and then back to his phone. Lauren has not responded to his latest text. Then, he realizes he has no reception. He holds his phone up to search for a signal, gets nothing, and looks down just in time.

"Jesus!"

Gil stops abruptly, skip-stepping backward as he trips and falls onto his ass, scooching away from the drop he nearly walked over. When he's sure of the ground beneath him, he leans forward to look over the ledge. It's an almost vertical drop littered with fallen tree limbs, forty feet down at least. A faint snap, like a branch breaking, sounds behind him as he stares over the intimidating cliff. He turns, crawling away from the ledge and peering into the impenetrable foliage. Another sound follows, this one almost like a moan. He imagines a huge, rotted tree, burdened by age, cracking under its own weight and crashing to the ground. For a few seconds, Gil holds his breath, waiting for more.

Nothing happens. The stillness resumes. The forest is unbearably calm. Though he tries to silence his thoughts, they come plodding unbidden into his mind.

The haunted mountain really is haunted…

But such thoughts should not be unwelcome. Like he told Lauren, *he wanted to believe, wished it was real.* If he's being honest with himself, he still does. Being here, sensing something extraordinary and unexplainable, this should be the best moment of Gil's life. So why does he feel so—

Something crawls over his skin. He shivers at the thought, at the ridiculous notion that any such thing could be true.

Ghosts. Poltergeists. The unjustly dead lying in eternal unrest. That crawling sensation again—

"Fuck!"

An enormous black spider scurries over the back of his hand, its two front legs drawn up defensively as it climbs up his wrist. He flicks his arm, sending the spider into a bush as he scrambles to his feet, momentarily forgetting about the ledge. Panicking, he spins around and tries to get his bearings, careful not to move too much in any direction. When he locates the cliff, he plants his feet and slides cautiously away. His shoes grind in the coarse dirt. He is crouched, peering all around for spiderwebs or hidden drop-offs.

Gil pats his pockets, checking that he still has his phone and the map. As he does, he sees a brightly lit area through the trees. After that series of minor frights, he had been prepared to start trekking back to Sunrise Hill. Instead, he makes another cursory check for spiderwebs, then plows through the thick underbrush, shoving branches out of his way and struggling to find footing until he emerges in a clearing.

Bright sunlight fills half of the open space. It enters at a sharp angle through a circular break in the tree cover, reminding Gil once again that the hour is growing late. Smiling and laughing, Gil jogs across the clearing toward the sunlight. As soon as he reaches it, clouds roll in and gloom settles over the forest. Though chills run down his spine, he heaves a sigh of relief. Standing in the clearing, free of the trail's claustrophobic confinement, Gil can finally breathe easy again. He feels as if he's just escaped the confines of a prison cell, and also like a bumbling fool who got himself worked up over an old wives' tale. He probably wasn't even that close to walking over that ledge. And the spider almost certainly wasn't venomous. This is precisely the reason he needs to be out here. He had been spineless his entire life. Even at a young age, he knew what his parents were up to, and he knew it was wrong. They were slimy opportunists who exploited people's fragile emotions for financial gain, and Gil had sat by, doing nothing. Leaving the way he did hasn't really changed anything. If he wants to start over, he has to begin by learning to stand up for himself. He has to trust his instincts and follow through with his beliefs.

But, also, he needs to keep his head on straight so he doesn't get lost on some sort of bitter journey of self-discovery.

Glancing around the circular clearing, Gil sees a broad trail to his left. To the best of his recollection, that is the direction he came from. Realizing he must have lost the main trail shortly after crossing the pass, he chuckles and starts in that direction, though his eyes linger on the curious arrangement of trees to the right.

Six large sycamores grow along that side of the clearing. The ground beneath the sycamores contains none of the tangled underbrush that covers the rest of the mountain. It almost looks like five paths fanning out from between the six trees. They are narrow and shaded from above, not as obvious as the trail to the left, but they do appear to be trails of a sort. Perhaps they were made by teenagers coming up here for a good time. Or they could be footpaths for scavenging animals —bears or mountain cats. Gil laughs again. He has no clue what kind of wildlife they have in the Adirondacks. Another topic to bring up with Lauren later.

Suppressing the urge to investigate, Gil continues toward

the trail leading back to Sunrise Hill. He does not want to get stuck up here after dark. Just before he leaves the clearing, he hears a new sound. He remembers the snapping branch he heard a few minutes before and the moaning that he assumed to be a creaking tree trunk. This, however, is a distinct scraping noise. Nothing natural about it, but rather human-like starts and stops with swift, clean swipes. A blade against wood.

Against his better judgment, Gil turns away from the trail. He stands before the line of sycamores, listening to gauge the direction of the scraping. The longer he stands there, the less sure he becomes. The five paths look identical. They might be one and the same, or they all might lead to dead ends.

For lack of a more definitive option, Gil steps onto the path between the third and fourth sycamores, treading as lightly and silently as he can.

6

THE SCRAPING GETS LOUDER as Gil moves deeper into the trees, confirming that he's chosen the correct path. But now that he's getting closer, he wishes he'd picked another one. Probably more sensible to approach from behind, spotting the scraper through the branches at a distance. Just to satisfy his curiosity. He has no great desire to put himself out there like this, engaging with some local as they go about their business.

No, he reminds himself. *That is precisely why I came here, to a small town in an unfamiliar part of the country. To put myself out there. To force myself to interact with real people. To be genuine and forthright. To learn how to make my way in regular society and stop hiding all the damn time.*

Gil pushes himself onward, then comes to a sudden halt when he notices a dark figure swaying between the branches. The scraping sound that drew him has ceased, but it must have been coming from there. He creeps forward a few more steps, taking pains to step soundlessly along the leaf-littered forest floor.

"Hullo."

Gil lets out a short, piercing yelp and jumps as he looks down to his left. His heart leaps in his chest.

The speaker sits on a log bench only a few paces away. How did Gil get so close without seeing the guy? The man has a short, bulky branch in one hand and a small utility knife in the other. He glances up, seemingly amused by Gil's fright. His hair and beard are mostly gray with streaks of white. He has a receding hairline but a full head of hair swept back in a natural wave. Even though he's seated, Gil can tell the man is tall and sturdily built, unaffected by the frailty that generally diminishes people his age.

When Gil doesn't say anything, the man turns his attention back to the knife and branch. "I'm guessin' that was you cursin' up a storm out there."

"Sorry, I..." Gil starts but can't find the words. He glances over his shoulder, staring at the shape he'd seen in the trees and realizing it's a black jacket hanging from a dead bough. "I didn't see you there."

"No," says the man, setting the knife into the branch. "No, you wouldn't. Not if you're not lookin'. Startled me yourself, with all that hollerin'. Not many folks come 'round this way." He carves at the wood, whittling out a wedge and then holding it up to inspect his notch. He sees Gil watching. "I sell them in town, but I carve them up here. So?"

"It's, uh...nice."

"Yeah," the man smirks. "But that's not what I meant. So, what're you doin' up here?"

"Oh," Gil laughs nervously and gazes over his shoulder toward the clearing. "I came out for a hike, but I...I'm not familiar with the trails. New here."

"That right? Where're you from?"

"California."

"Whereabouts?" The man whittles out another chunk.

"It's a...a small community. You wouldn't know it."

Without emotion, the man looks up from his whittling. "Try me."

"Well... Santa Rosa."

"Santa Rosa, huh? Ain't that small. Here, kid. Have a seat." The man slides over, making space for Gil on the log. "Name's Wesley. Friends call me Wes."

Gil hesitates before slipping off his backpack and sitting down. "I'm Gil. You know Santa Rosa?"

"Sure. Up in wine country." Wes nods and chips away at the branch. "That means you're runnin'. From what?"

Glancing up sharply, Gil stares defiantly at the man. Wes continues working the branch. He looks at Gil sidewise, grinning and raising his eyebrows, never missing a beat with the knife. Gil takes a deep breath and reminds himself once more why he's here.

No more hiding.

"My parents," Gil admits, trying to keep a steady voice. "They're...they're really terrible people."

"Little old to be going through a rebellious phase, aren'cha?"

"No, it's not..." Gil sighs. "Yes, you're right. But I was too scared to stand up for myself as a teenager. To do what I knew was right."

"Are you still?"

"I'm trying to change. I'll always be partly responsible. And I'll have to live with that. But I don't want to be that way anymore."

"Good for you. What was it? Smuggling? Dope?"

Gil shakes his head. "They took money from people—a lot of people—by pretending to be something they're not. Gained people's trust and used that to manipulate them. *'Invest in this. Fund this venture. Triple your money in two years.'* That sort of thing. They destroyed lives and ruined families and never showed a shred of remorse. Not even after they were caught."

"But they *were* caught?"

Gil nods meekly. "Most of what they did fell into legal loopholes. Morally, I guess it was always going to catch up to them... to us. I just wish I'd done something sooner. I could have put a stop to it years ago, but I didn't. How many people could I have helped? When they finally got caught, it came down on all of us. Me and my sister, we're not culpable for anything, but we're linked by association. Our names dragged through the mud, our pictures pasted all over the internet and local media. Someone got ahold of a family photo and put it on a billboard in San Francisco. So, yes, I am running. I had to get away from that. From them. Just wanted to disappear and start a new life."

Wes whittles in silence for a few moments, his head

bobbing in thoughtful contemplation. With one eye, he peeks at Gil.

"Sounds like you're doin' all you can. That's enough. My old man used to beat all hell outta me. I had black eyes and bruised ribs all the way up until I split at fifteen. It was hard the first few years, bein' on my own, but I made my way. Ended up out West. In those days, transient livin' only took us west. Took whatever work I could. Up and down the coast, from Seattle to Tijuana. Used to work the fields at a vineyard just outside St Helena, so I spent plenty of weekends gettin' drunk in Santa Rosa."

"I have friends in St Helena. Or, I used to..."

"Always new folks around to serve that purpose."

"Yeah..."

Gil jerks upright when a hawk shrieks overhead. Several crows call in response. Dark shapes move among the branches.

"Don't be so jumpy, kid. A lot of wildlife on this mountain. Won't do you no harm. Nothin' to worry about."

"Have you lived in Pickett's Post long?"

"I used to, but not anymore. Got a little place down the other side of the mountain. After a few years out West, I got fed up. Not unlike you, but my gripes were mostly with the hippies. Then, when I came here, I had problems with the yuppies up from the city. Turns out I just got a general dislike for people."

"Sorry, should I...?"

"Not what I meant, kid. I got no issue with meetin' folks like you. Pleasant conversation. It's when they gather in groups. Bullyin' behavior. I got fed up, went away for a while. But, of all the places I've been, people around these parts were always the most agreeable. The locals, that is. Tend to mind their business, and they're honest. So, I came back. Just don't want to get too close, if you know what I mean. I got one friend left from my days in Pickett's Post. She comes around once a week to bring me supplies and pick up my carvings. Sells them out of her shop."

"I think I saw her…" Gil mutters, almost as if he's speaking to himself. "An old woman? Carrying a canvas bag?"

Smirking, Wes eyes Gil from head to toe. "If you wanna be accepted around here as a local, don't be so nosy."

"I didn't mean to…I just…I passed her on my way up…"

"I don't mind." Wes rests his hands on his knees. "Just some friendly advice." He gazes around the forest, takes a few deep breaths, and then peers closely at Gil.

Intimidated by the old man's searching gaze, Gil looks away, letting his eyes roam. The crows have settled in the branches. The jacket hanging nearby has stopped swaying.

Without looking at Wes, Gil asks, "Do you come up here often?"

"Just about every day for more'n a year now. It's quiet. Peaceful. Sometimes, I'll hear folks trudging through the trails. They never stay long."

"Why not?"

"You don't know?"

"A friend told me the mountain's supposed to be haunted."

"Ain't that reason enough?"

"Do you believe it?"

"Not a word of it. Nothin' up here but an old man and his thoughts."

Gil smiles and nods. He looks down at his feet, glances at Wes's carving, and sweeps his eyes around the woods. "How far is the peak from here?" he asks, attempting to change the subject.

Wes sniggers. "So, that's it, is it? You want to know."

"Sorry? Know what?"

Wes turns his body to face Gil squarely. His eyebrows bounce in a suggestive dance. "You want to know what it feels like."

With his eyes trained sharply on Gil, Wes raises his branch, wraps his fingers around it, and squeezes. He wrings his hands in cartoonish mimicry of a strangling, his tongue lolling from the corner of his mouth. Wes stops when Gil starts to squirm uncomfortably, but then he takes his knife, sneering as he slashes across his branch like slicing into a throat. And finally, he raises the branch high above his head, drilling into Gil's wide eyes with a piercing stare as he brings the branch repeatedly downward at full force.

Gil's mouth hangs open. His eyes dart from the ground to Wes to his backpack, from the hanging jacket to the direction of the sycamores and the clearing, and then above to the rapidly diminishing daylight.

"Relax," Wes laughs and sets down the knife and branch. "I'm just foolin' with you. You're gonna have to forgive my sick old sense of humor. Them murders, they happened a long time ago."

Nervous laughter sputters from Gil's mouth as he tries to regain his composure. His heart rate is up, and he worries the reverberations might travel along the log, alerting Wes to his weakness.

"I don't know anything about the murders," says Gil. "I heard it was haunted; that's all. When I was younger, I was fascinated with haunted houses and abandoned asylums.

Ghosts, possessions, curses, stuff like that. Since I'm living in the presence of an allegedly haunted place, I thought I owed it to myself to give it a shot. Needed some time with my thoughts, anyhow."

"Well, this is the place for that," Wes nods approvingly. "Not haunted, though."

"You don't get a strange feeling here? Like something's off?"

"What's the matter? You got the spooks?"

"Kind of, yeah," admits Gil.

"Ah, don't be so simple-minded, kid. You seem bright. Should know there's no such thing. Ghosts, spirits, souls— what are they but your own memories? The life you've lived? Wishes. Hopes and fears. Guilt. Regrets. When we die, they die with us."

"What makes you so sure?"

"I'll tell you what it is that's givin' you the creeps; it's these trails. On this mountain, the forest is dense and dark and tricky as all hell. More'n a few people have gotten themselves lost and stuck up here overnight. It scares folks, and for good reason, but there ain't nothin' supernatural about it. Just nature Herself, doin' what She's always done."

Gil's tension begins to release. He nods at Wes with a small smile. "You're right. Maybe that's all I needed. Some time out in nature. To be present and aware of myself. Ever since I decided to leave home, I've wondered whether I truly know myself at all. Who am I? What do I want? Where do I belong? But I've been hinging on the past, trying so hard to separate myself from it that I can't appreciate the world as it is. Here and now. It's like I'm still a boy trying to spot a ghost, searching for proof of an afterlife or evidence of mythical creatures, when, really, I ought to be getting to know myself. And standing up for what I believe in."

"'Atta boy!" Wes unexpectedly claps Gil on the shoulder, and Gil cannot believe the strength he feels in that hand. "That's what these woods're meant for. Reflections upon yerself. Identify your flaws, own up to 'em, and then do somethin' about it."

"Now that I'm here, I don't even know what I would do if I saw a ghost. I don't have the slightest clue how I'd react."

"Maybe worry about that another time, kid. The sun's dyin' down. It'll sink fast now. It don't get any easier up here, the long, dark night. You know the way out?"

"I think I can retrace my steps."

"Didn't you hear what I said? Even if you find a trail, they're misleadin'. Almost aggressively so. If you don't know where you're steppin', it's not only tricky, it's downright dangerous."

The light has dimmed considerably. The leafy treetops make it hard to tell, but Gil assumes the sun is already hidden behind the mountain and nearing the horizon. His phone says it's almost six-thirty. He holds it up to search for reception, but the bars remain stubbornly empty.

Wesley shakes his head with bemusement. "Don't expect that thing to help."

With a sigh, Gil puts the phone away. "How long does it take to get down?"

"Can't go back the way you came up. Dark'll be on you before you make it halfway. Wouldn't want to be navigatin' the pass without your eyes. Unless... Weather's not too bad tonight. You prepared to camp it? What you got in that bag?"

"An empty water bottle, a book, and a shirt," Gil says, his shoulders slumping.

"Not even a flashlight," Wes grunts as he stands up. "Let me grab my jacket."

"You don't have to," Gil stammers, rising to his feet. "Really, don't bother. I don't want to put you out. I'll just... uh..."

"It's no bother, kid. I know the way, and you don't. Need to be gettin' on myself anyhow."

As Wes plods toward the tree where his jacket hangs, Gil cannot help but feel self-conscious and insignificant. Wes is broad-shouldered and must stand well over six feet. Gil slings his backpack over his shoulders, watching as Wes nudges something on the ground with his foot. While Gil waits, he takes a closer look at the whittled branch. He tries to distinguish a shape, but he can't decide whether it's supposed to be a person or an animal. Perhaps a mix of both? He leans closer, noticing how its face is contorted, its mouth wrenched open in a wail of pain or terror.

"Would you like to see?"

Gil jumps at the sound of Wes's voice. He backs up and turns around, slamming directly into the man. It feels like walking into a tree trunk.

"No... No, that's okay. But what is it?"

"A mythical creature," Wes says with a grin. He walks ahead and calls to Gil without turning back. "Better move along."

"What about your things?" Gil says, glancing down at the knife and branch. "Are you just gonna leave them here?"

"Nobody comes up here, remember? If they do happen to disappear, well... I'll remember your face."

. . .

7

Though Wesley had started off leading Gil back toward the clearing, he'd veered into the woods before reaching it. They've been moving slowly through a dense thicket, and Gil has lost all sense of direction. There's still some light, but not much. Every once in a while, Wes will call back in a low, unaffected tone, telling Gil to look out for a branch, a root, or a ditch. And he keeps reminding Gil to stick close, to keep his eyes sharp.

Gil feels conflicted. He's glad he ran into Wes and that Wes is willing to guide him out. But now he's wishing more than ever that he'd turned back sooner.

"I can't see the trail at all," announces Gil.

"We're not on a trail. This is a shortcut. I prefer to stay off the main paths. They were designed to be confusing. This way's faster if you know what you're doin'."

"It all looks the same." Gil starts to breathe heavily. "You're sure this leads back to town?"

Wes answers with a grunt. "Came up this side of the mountain often enough when I lived in Pickett's Post. I know this mountain better'n anybody. Now, you be careful from here on, you hear? Couple'a steep drops comin' up. Stick close. Keep me in your sight."

"I can't see a thing."

"Just step where I step and you'll be alright."

They continue without speaking for a while, the forest growing dimmer by the minute. Wes doesn't mention the fading light, but he seems to pick up the pace rather than slow down out of caution.

"Wouldn't it be easier if you cleared out a trail?" asks Gil.

"Sure it would," grumbles Wes. "But that would be like an invitation. It's been nice talkin' with you, kid, but I don't need a bunch of doe-eyed ghost hunters and murder-mystery types swarmin' my sanctuary day and night. Know what I mean?"

Gil nods even though Wes hasn't turned to look at him.

The path is primarily level. They've only descended at a few points. Despite the chill in the air, the constant batting away of branches keeps Gil plenty warm. Sweat drips down the back of his neck.

"Were you around when the murders occurred?" says Gil.

Wes doesn't answer right away. He doesn't stop walking, but his steps seem to slow.

"I was."

"What do you know about them?"

"Most folks around here know some. Why don't you ask a friend when you get down?"

"I only have one friend..." Gil says, mostly to himself. "Is it true that the bodies were never found?"

"Far as I know."

"And you've never...you know?"

"What?"

"Found anything...weird?"

"Weird?"

This brings Wes to a halt. He stands motionless for a moment, then turns to face Gil. He steps closer, staring at Gil with cold, inquisitive eyes. He smirks, shakes his head, and claps Gil on the shoulder before turning around. They keep walking, veering slightly to the right.

Wes's pace has increased again. It's getting more difficult for Gil to keep up. He keeps losing Wes in the shadows ahead.

Suddenly, Wes says, "I know where the bodies are."

Gil stops, staring at Wes's shoulders. "You've...seen them?"

"I have," answers Wes, pausing and half-turning to peer back at Gil. "Anything else?" he says, allowing Gil no more than two seconds to respond. "Then I suggest we keep movin'."

Wes starts off again at once, but Gil hangs back. He's starting to feel a nagging unease. He doesn't like being off the trails. It doesn't feel as though they're descending quickly enough, or at all. As grateful as he is to Wes, he's beginning to wonder whether any of this is a good idea.

But at this point, he doesn't have any other choice. Full dark will be upon them in a matter of minutes, the forest is the densest he's seen all day, and he has no sense of where he might be on the mountain.

He takes out his phone, sees that it's almost half past seven.

About to turn on the flashlight, Gil realizes he's getting reception. Only one bar, but that's a good sign. It means they're headed in the right direction.

Then, he sees that he has thirteen missed text messages.

"Stay with me, kid. Like a..." Wes calls from ahead, but his words trail off.

"Like a what?" Gil says as he stares at the screen.

"I said, like a spirit, kid."

"I'm coming." Gil darts forward a few steps and turns on his phone's flashlight.

"Turn that thing off," says Wes. "As long as you stay near,

you won't need it. It'll only cast shadows. Makes it harder to see, not easier."

"Are you sure?"

"I've been comin' up here since before you were born, kid. Know this mountain like my own backyard. Be careful up here around this bend."

Reluctantly, Gil switches off the flashlight. The glow of his screen illuminates his face. He trips over a fallen branch. As soon as he steadies himself, another branch smacks him in the face.

"You alright back there?" asks Wes.

"Yeah, I'm fine. It's just...can you slow down?"

"Night's nippin' at our heels. Best not tempt fate. Ain't that what they say?"

"Who?" asks Gil, squinting ahead to find Wes, who only chuckles in response to the question. His enormous bulk is no longer visible in the gloom. "Shit..." Gil stops to get his bearings. He holds up his phone again, opens the unread messages. All thirteen of them are from Lauren.

5:59 - Gil! get out of there!

6:00 - my friend saw your pic and freaked!

6:02 - she told me the guy was released last year

6:05 - there's a rumor that he came back here and

6:06 - lives in the woods outside town

6:09 - omg gil i'm so sorry

6:10 - i swear i thought he died in jail

6:12 - his name is wesley hall, they let him out on a tech-
    nicality

6:14 - he might still go to that mountain

6:17 - write back asap

6:29 - gil are you okay???
6:48 - this isn't funny gil, please write back
7:01 - Gil!?!?

A deathly silence washes over him. The forest seems to have swallowed Gil. He hears his heartbeat and Wes's receding footsteps crunching in the fallen leaves. Then, the footsteps stop. Gil takes a single deep breath and is shocked by how obscenely loud it is. Around him, he sees only the vaguest suggestions of trees and branches. Above, narrow glimpses of a leaden sky. He doesn't know whether to confront Wes or turn around and start running. If he runs, he'll lose his way immediately. Wes might be his only chance to get down.

Then again, Wes might not be leading him down at all.

As Gil considers how to respond to Lauren, a single footstep crunches the leaves ahead. He looks up, peering into the darkness. After a long pause, another crunch. Before Gil can type out a message, his phone lets out a shrill *DING*.

"What was that." Wes's question, inflected like a statement, reaches Gil as a whisper.

"Damnit," Gil mutters. His hands tremble. He nearly drops his phone. His eyes have trouble focusing.

7:28 - i'm coming to find you

Gil looks up and feels like he's in a cage. He spins around, his mind racing as he tries to make a decision. Every alarm bell in his system is clanging. What has he done? How can he get out? What would his parents do? He knows exactly what they would do. They would lie and scheme their way out, smooth-talking all the way down to the trailhead and back to town. Suddenly, their immoralities don't seem quite so bad. Useful even. Maybe he should have paid more attention. He could have learned a few things. Picked up a few tools. Instead, he's helpless. He's been stunned by the Siren's song, and now—

"You comin' or what, kid?"

"Uh...yeah. I just had to answer a text. Coming. Sorry, I can't see you. Where are you?"

Still staring at his phone screen, Gil finishes typing his reply. He starts walking in the direction he thinks Wes's voice came from. Just as he's about to press *Send*, his foot comes down on nothing. He lets out a meaningless groan and tumbles forward into the darkness.

8

GIL STANDS at a high ledge overlooking a rocky shore below. He recognizes the place, knows he's been here before, but can't quite grasp how he got here. Wasn't he...someplace else? He can't recall, but he feels like he was supposed to have left this place behind.

So what is he doing here?

He steps closer. His toes dangle over the edge, but he feels secure. A soft breeze sweeps in. It swirls around him, cooling his skin and whipping his hair, though never threatening his balance. A stunning view stretches across his field of vision. Pure white lumps of cloud drift across a pastel sky. The sea reflects the sky's color, broken by long, slow-moving white caps. Rocky, pine-covered islands rise far out in the water.

Giant sea birds soar above. The boulders below are cut with a sculptor's tools and arranged with an artist's eye for precision. To the right and left, the cliff stretches as far as he can see. Olive trees grow in the distance, reaching out over the edge toward the expansive blue horizon.

What a life this could be. Solitude and serenity. Perhaps he should consider remaining here this time. He can live in the wilderness, scavenging like our prehistoric forebears. Over time, he could fashion a hovel, building it up year by year until it resembles a home. A seaside cabin. All the olives and fish and seafowl he can catch. No need to worry about facing others or confronting his compromised scruples.

Whispers reach Gil, carried on a breeze growing subtly stronger. He cannot make out words, but the whispers contain urgency, desperation, panic. It sounds like multiple voices, all murmuring at the same time, far away and from all directions. Some come from the bottom of the cliff, some from the sea, others from above or behind. The wind picks up, making it impossible to distinguish one voice from the next. Then, Gil hears his name. It's faint at first, just as muddled as the whispers. Each time it repeats, it grows louder. This is not a whisper but a scream, rapidly approaching from a great distance. He recognizes the voice but cannot attach it to a face, just like he is not yet sure where he is or why he's here. And then, a tug on his loins. A memory. Of ecstasy.

It's Lauren's voice.

Calling out to him.

Begging.

The whispers grow louder as dark clouds roll in. The sunlight diminishes. The sea darkens until it's almost black.

Gusts shove him this way and that. He spreads his feet and lowers his center of balance, but the wind keeps him from stepping away from the ledge.

In between screams, Lauren moans with pleasure. He remembers being with her, feeling her body writhe beneath his, the warmth of her breath, the cushion of her breasts.

She screams again, no trace of pleasure this time, but rather a razor blade shriek of imminent terror. The scream comes from behind. He turns, intending to rush to her side. He'll do whatever is necessary to protect her.

But he halts before he's even started. Ten feet away, a gigantic bird sits perched on a mound. The feathers on its back and wings are black. Everything else is rusty orange, with white around its red eyes and gray streaks on its head. Blood and gore drip from its beak and talons as it digs voraciously into a mutilated pile of carrion. It looks like a bearded vulture, but it's larger than any bird Gil can imagine. One great eye watches Gil as the bird probes through the flesh, pulling out a long strand of innards. It swallows a liver with one gulp and stands erect, as tall as a person.

For a long time, it scrutinizes Gil, its eyes warning him off. If he attempts to back away, he'll plunge over the cliff. So, he remains still, watching in horror as the bird judges him.

Finally, it returns to its meal. It pulls and tears with its talons before jabbing its beak into the bloated carcass. Gil can hear the flesh tearing. As the bird tugs at a piece of scalp, Gil sees the blood-stained strands of hair attached to it.

Blonde hair.

Lauren.

"No!"

Gil braces himself against the violent gusts and lunges

forward. The bird hears him and spreads its wings, showing off a wingspan as long as a limousine.

Before Gil reaches the bird, a deafening scream rends the air. A sharp, high-pitched wail that feels like long needles inserted into his ear canals. He covers his ears, but it hardly makes a difference. The scream continues, growing louder still, throwing off his balance, making him want to retch up his insides. Soon, he's screaming, too. He knows the noise is coming from the vulture, but when he glances up, the bird's beak is clamped around a scrap of flesh. Confused, Gil pulls his hands away from his head, and the unending screech instantly brings him to his knees.

The bird's head twists, spinning around until it's facing backward like an owl. The back of its head reveals a woman's face. Exotic, ravishing features. She is more beautiful and sensuous than any woman Gil has ever seen.

Gil forgets about Lauren. He wants nothing more from this life than to possess the elusive, bestial woman before him. He will do anything. He will willingly offer himself. He will be her carrion just to get closer. But it's her voice that's keeping him away. Her mouth is spread wide, the paralyzing scream issuing from deep within. A scream that, if it goes on much longer, will make Gil throw himself over the cliff, praying that the rocks below kill him swiftly, mercifully.

And hoping that this Siren will feast on him in death.

9

GIL'S HEAD IS THROBBING. He tries to sit up, but aches surface all over his body. Giving up, he falls back, and his head slams onto a hard surface. Slowly, his eyes focus. But where is he? Another dream?

Turning to his left, he sees a spray of blonde hair beside him, almost glowing in the low light.

"Lauren..." he utters with a sigh of relief.

He's in bed, waking from a nightmare that spanned an entire day. That must be it. After Lauren told him about the haunted mountain, they had sex again and fell asleep, her story worming its way deep into his subconscious only to burst through the thin veneer of sleep, taking on the terrifying shades of reality.

He squeezes his eyes shut, pleading for this to be true, wishing desperately that the stones poking into his back are only remnants of the dream.

But the scent of earth and dead leaves, the sharp lines of the moonlit clouds, the chirping of crickets, the distant call of an owl—all these things tell him otherwise.

Can he still be on the haunted mountain? Mount Tomb? And what is Lauren doing here? Why are they sleeping on the ground?

Achingly, Gil raises himself onto an elbow. Her hair is fanned out in the dirt. A few long strands cover her face. As he slides closer, he winces at a sharp pang in his side. He grasps Lauren's shoulder, but she doesn't stir.

"Lauren. Lauren, wake up..." Running his fingers through her hair, he leans close and whispers into her ear. "Lauren, get up. We have to—"

When he untangles his fingers, he notices a subtle shimmer, a reflection of the moonlight. A cool, slippery substance drips down his palm onto his wrist and forearm.

"What..."

Gil falls back and frantically slides away. A biting pain in his right leg travels up his body. He groans, letting his leg go limp as he struggles to drag himself with arms that feel battered and tender.

What happened? He'd wanted to head back when he met that old man, Wes, who offered to show him the way. But the old man took him off the trails. They'd been forcing their way through thick growth. Wes had...confessed? Or something had alarmed Gil? And then his phone. No flashlights—*they make it harder to see*—what the hell kind of advice is that? The messages from Lauren. Wesley Hall. Pickett's Curse. Released on a technicality and free to...

"No... No, no, no, no... Lauren..."

Finally, Gil manages to sit up. He expects to find that he's surrounded by dense forest, but he's not. Moonlight from a gap overhead offers limited visibility, and he recognizes this place. Behind him are the six sycamores, standing like sentinels on guard. To his left is the one trail he's seen on this mountain, which may or may not lead back to the pass and Sunrise Hill. Beyond the clearing, total darkness blankets the forest.

Gil takes a moment to look himself over. His arms are scratched and bruised. There are throbbing welts on his head, cuts on his cheeks, and a split in his lip. Blood drips from his nose. Each time he discovers a new wound, his eyes are drawn back to Lauren. He wants to turn her over for a closer look; he wants to carry her to a hospital; he wants to shake her until she wakes up. But he's afraid of what he'll find if he touches her.

"You shouldn't be here... You shouldn't be here..." he

mutters, choking on the saliva suddenly coating his mouth and throat.

When he attempts to stand up, the pain in his leg becomes so intense that it simply gives out beneath him. He crumples down, tumbling forward and falling over Lauren's body. For a few seconds, he remains there, his face planted into her abdomen, his arms draped over her chest and thighs, unable to decide whether to curl up beside her or get up and run into the darkness. Her flesh is frigid. There is no rise or fall in her chest. Gil's breathing grows erratic and labored as he pushes away from her.

"Lauren, why? You shouldn't... What happened? No. Fuck. Oh, Jesus. Lauren..."

Gil scrambles away and his leg gives out again. He feels around for a broken bone, then tries once more. This time, he suffers through the pain, grunting and groaning until he's up. He puts most of his weight on his good leg. When he tries walking, he curses with each half-step. Saliva floods his mouth; red droplets spray from his lips as he fights through the agony.

Staring down at Lauren's lifeless body, he reels with intense regret as he realizes he has no way of getting her off the mountain. There is no guarantee he'll be able to get himself off Mount Tomb, but she does not deserve to be stuck up here. Limping around the clearing, racking his brain for an idea, for something to help him, Gil hears a sound.

Scraping.

The same scraping he heard earlier. Before he met—

"It's you..." Gil growls. "You..."

The scraping seems to come from all directions. Gil hobbles back and forth, peering into the surrounding darkness. Each time he puts weight on his injured leg, a feral grunt rises from his throat. When the scraping intensifies, he stops and glares into the trees. His wheezing breaths make it difficult to hear.

"What have you done?" Gil roars. "Why her? Why didn't you kill me? *I said why?!*"

The scraping continues. It gets faster, louder, more vigorous. Then, abruptly, it stops.

"Thought you deserved a chance…" Wesley's voice issues from the darkness. Same as the scraping, it's impossible to tell where it's coming from.

Gil twists this way and that, wincing and moaning but always sticking close to Lauren's body.

"A chance? A chance for what?"

"Odd as it sounds, you made a believer outta me."

"What?"

"I tell you what, kid—people can change. They can. You can. After all those years, I learned remorse. I did. That festerin' need within me up and vanished. Locked up for thirty-one years, been on the outside just over a year now, and I never once felt that old, familiar urge. Even comin' up here every day, whilin' away my dyin' years in this shrine to my crimes, I did not feel the call. A reformed man. Remade. Cleansed. Livin' an honest life. No longer a slave to that need. To hear them beg. To hold life in my hands and feel it…pass on. The smell of blood. Of death."

"Bullshit," snaps Gil. He coughs and spits blood, still glaring into the trees and still unable to place the voice.

"Then you turn up," Wes ignores the interruption. "You waltz in here, where few dare to tread, bringin' your ghouls and your stupidity…your fear. I was only tryin' to help, kid. Trust me, I wanted you outta here more'n you did. And I told you to put the goddamn phone away. Told you to stick close and watch out for them drop-offs, didn't I? *Didn't I?!*"

Wesley's voice rises to an angry pitch, pulling Gil's head around toward the row of sycamores. But when Wes continues, his voice is low again and blends into the rustling leaves.

"I found you at the bottom of that cliff face, bruised and unconscious and tangled in a thicket. I brought you back to safety. I *helped* you. But then *she* turns up, stompin' onto *my mountain*, shriekin' like a maniac in the silent night. Spent years nurturin' a peace and quiet of my own, and then *POOF!* Gone. The stupidity. The fear. The ghost…"

"There are no ghosts!" Gil is panting from the pain of holding himself erect, the hopelessness of the situation. "You said so yourself! There's only you!"

"Yes… Yes, that's what I thought. And I believed it. That's how it was when I brought them bodies up here. Did what I had to do. Hid them where they'd never be found. But you… and she…convinced me…"

The scraping resumes. Gil spins around, searching frantically, spittle spraying from his mouth with each raspy breath. He trips over Lauren's body and yells out in pain as he falls to his knees.

"You showed me…"

"Showed you what?" Gil grunts and picks himself up.

"The ghosts, kid. They're real. Sure as shit. You brought 'em out, set them on me like a vulture. Here I am, an old man breathin' his last breaths. Can't have many years left in me. A few, but not enough. I rotted away all those years in a concrete hell, thinkin' I'd been rehabilitated. Thinkin' I could treat ordinary folks with fairness and respect. Delusions, kid. They've been here all along, workin' on me. Wraiths of the human race. My own creations. You and that girl—she's a pretty one, ain't she? A nice addition to my collection. You two finally opened this old man's eyes. Helped me to see what's always been here. Would you like to see, too?"

Gil finally stops spinning. He's staring down at Lauren. He wants to reach down and brush the hair from her face, but it hurts just to bend over. Heaving panicked breaths, he stares from the trail to the sycamores. Above, clouds cover the moon, rendering the clearing almost as dark as the trees.

"Don't you understand, kid? I'm offerin' you exactly what you came lookin' for. This is what you wanted. Ghosts're real, and you drew 'em out of their hidin' place. This is all because of you."

"You killed her! Not me!"

"You, me, the ghosts of Mount Tomb—all the same in the end."

"What do you want?"

"What do I want? You still don't understand what I'm sayin', do you? This isn't about me. It's about you. You came up here, spoutin' your nonsense and askin' your questions, and I set you straight. Thought I did, anyway. Turns out you were right, kid. That's what I'm trying to tell you. I'm thankin' you. You might not be happy about what I did to your friend there, but consider this—if I wanted to kill you, I would have done it the moment you intruded upon my solitude. I may be old, but I don't think I'd have trouble with a scrawny fella like yerself. Instead, I listened to your nonsense and even offered to bring you to safety, asking nothing in return. When you still didn't trust me, wouldn't listen, and fell over that cliff, I could have left you to die a slow, agonizing death of starvation. I saved you, but all that time, I was thinkin'...thinkin' that maybe there is somethin' special about this here mountain. Some kinda magic that I helped to unleash. The ghosts were already workin' on me. Well, when this yapperin' bitch came intrudin' where she don't belong, them ghosts took hold. They came to life, and my better nature was restored. I thirsted for killin', the ghosts thirsted for a companion...*and still I let you live!* An expression of gratitude. Do you see? Do you understand how the world works yet? I'm offerin' you a choice."

"Why?" Gil says plaintively.

"You made me see that this mountain *is* haunted. That ghosts *are* real. Because of you, I will enjoy the final years of my life. Call it gratitude. Or call it punishment if that makes it easier to wrap your head around. I don't give a good goddamn what you call it. Even men like me have honor. And, if you haven't figured it out yet, I'm helpin' you to become a man. I heard your story, and I like you, kid. So, I put you in a position where you *have to choose.* There's no runnin' across the country this time. No sidesteppin' what's lyin' right in front of you."

"This isn't a choice! She's dead!"

"Yes...she is that." The scraping stops as Wes lets out a curiously merry laughter. "But you're not. Not yet. So make your choice, kid."

The scraping resumes.

"What choice?!"

"Behind you."

Gil spins around, staring into the pitch-black wall of trees.

"That's the way off the mountain," says Wes. "It's dark. It's dangerous. Your friend there was wise enough to bring a flashlight, which may have helped you. Unfortunately, it broke when I beat her to death with it. Sorry 'bout that. If you choose to risk the hike down from here, I will not follow. Have faith. As for the girl...they will never find her body. Same as the others."

Staggering, panting, Gil drags his feet toward the trail. It presents a daunting, impenetrable darkness.

"But you need to ask yourself a question, kid. Will they blame you for her disappearance? Will you blame yourself? The memory of what you've done here—the ghost—will haunt you until your dying day. Believe me."

"Haunt me?" shouts Gil. He stops and spins around again, glancing at Lauren's body and feeling like he might be sick. He wants to curl into the fetal position by her side. To remain with her always. In truth, he hardly knows her, yet he feels attached. He feels responsible.

And he should have listened to her.

"Do not deny that you played a part in this. You can't be that ignorant. Go on. Get out of here. Try to forget your role in this. Try, if you dare..." The scraping stops. "Finished."

"What's finished?"

Something flies out from between the last two sycamores. The small object tumbles across the clearing, coming to rest in the spray of Lauren's hair. Gil limps forward and picks up a small figurine carved from wood.

The clouds have moved along. Moonlight once again fills

the clearing. Glimmers reflect in the pool of blood at Gil's feet.

The figurine has a long body and wings half-folded onto its back. At first, Gil thinks it's supposed to be an angel, except the face is anything but angelic. The eyes and mouth are wrenched wide with frenzied hysteria. And the legs are avian. They're long and scaly, with three forward-facing toes and one shorter rear toe, all equipped with massive pointed talons.

A Siren.

Gil looks up sharply at the spot where the figurine emerged. He holds it up and steps toward the sycamores. "How did you know? How did you know about this?"

Wes laughs. "How d'you think, kid? Your ghosts told me."

"No..."

"There's your proof. You're holdin' it in your hand. But if that's not enough, then you can come this way and see the ghost with your own eyes. Here and now, no more runnin'. It's yours for the takin'. Yes, you're injured. Yes, you'll have to fight an old man. I can tell you're afraid. But knowledge comes at a cost. Nothin's free. Maybe you never learned that lesson because of your folks. Well, I'm offerin' it to you now. Come this way. Confront me. Confront your fears. Can't be any worse than tryin' to limp down the mountain on your own, carryin' all that guilt on your shoulders. Come and meet your ghosts, kid."

The figurine's haunting expression reminds Gil of the delirious dream he woke from a few minutes ago. He'd been dreaming of that cliff ever since he brought the preserved foot home from Greece, believing the hawker's tale with all the ignorant enthusiasm of adolescence. Like everything else in his life, that trip had been paid for by his parents' illicit activities, and the money he'd used to purchase the foot had come from that same tainted pot.

Tension tightens every muscle in Gil's body. The panic has left him. He understands his position, but that doesn't make it any easier to commit. He takes deep, heavy breaths, shifting his gaze from the trail to the sycamores, from the Siren to Lauren's corpse, from the blood on his hand to his injured leg. After a while, he begins to pace, circling around her body and considering everything Wesley has said in spite of himself. How could Wes accurately peg the problems plaguing Gil's life after a twenty-minute conversation? How could he penetrate Gil's dreams and deepest fears? The longer Gil considers these things, the more resentful he becomes— and not just toward Wes. All the resentments of Gil's life rise fuming to the surface. He came to the Adirondacks to escape all that, but it has followed him here anyway. Perhaps he brought it with him through his unwillingness to leave those childish obsessions behind and truly start from nothing.

Wesley is right. Lauren's blood is both literally and figuratively on Gil's hands. Such things are not washed away so easily. You accept them. You adapt. You live with it any way you can. And maybe that means spending the rest of your life, no matter how much time you have left, trying to make it right.

Gil stares at the Siren. He can still hear its intoxicating scream, and he realizes it has always been there. The Siren's scream has been ringing in his head ever since he was a kid. Rather than fleeing from it, he might as well embrace it. He fiddles with the figurine, trying to find the best way to grasp it, the most effective way to inflict harm with it. When he has it firmly gripped, he takes a deep breath and limps toward the last sycamore.

As he slips between the tree trunks, drawn on by Wesley Hall's churning laughter, the trail connecting him to the world recedes. But all it promises is a dark, haunted life. At least, this way, Gil will have an opportunity to lay one ghost to rest.

In Case of Emergency

The kid stands in the middle of the bus, blocking the space by the exit doors. He's swiveling, jerking, strutting, undulating. His arms are eels, his waist a damaged hinge, his head bobbling like it's detached.

Tamara glances up from her phone and watches the little boy with mild amusement that draws ever nearer to irritation. He's been doing this peculiar dance since the last stop, right there in everybody's way. He might be six and he might be twelve. She can't tell. Her entire experience with kids comes from her cousin's children, whom she's only met a handful of times, and all she remembers is their bitching and complaining about every little thing—at a goddamn Christmas gathering! What kind of rotten, shitty kids can't find something to be happy about on Christmas Eve? Tamara's cousin, Gloria, is only a year older than her and has already created two monsters.

It's funny how Tamara used to look up to Gloria. Funny or

pathetic? Nowadays, she does not envy her cousin. Not one bit. Whenever Gloria's name comes up, she changes the subject. If Gloria and her kids are going to be at the family cookout, then it's *Sorry, I can't make it.*

That ill-fated Christmas party was the last time Tamara saw Gloria and...what's her husband's name? Ted? Fred? Bread? He's about as interesting as a piece of bread, anyway. Stale, white bread with furry signs of mold. And those bratty kids? Chip and Lucy? Mark and Cissy? Scum and Scummy, if Tamara is dishing out names.

The bus lurches to a jerky stop at the corner of Fifth and Washington. The driver pumps the brakes, and that final pump whips Tamara so far forward she almost spills off the seat. Her phone slips from her hand, but she just barely catches it, squeezing with fumbling fingers that swipe her back to the home screen. Grumbles of agitation rise from the other passengers. She expects someone to cuss out the driver. No one does.

It must have started raining. Why else would the driver pump the brakes like that? But when she looks, the windows are dry. So are the cars passing on the left and the people piled around the bus stop to the right.

Only two passengers hop onto the bus. It's not a very frequented route. The first, a young girl wearing entirely too much makeup, takes a seat near the front. The second is an old woman. No, an *ancient* woman. She hobbles down the aisle, searching for a seat, tilted off balance by a tote bag over-flowing with groceries. There's a free spot near the exit door, but the woman just stands before it.

Tamara stares for a moment before realizing the seat is not empty. That boy is standing on it. He's still doing his obnoxious little dance, kind of swiveling his hips, worm-like, with his face plastered against the window. Is he licking it? *Gross.* Or, no, maybe he's sticking his tongue out at the passengers of that military-green SUV. Meanwhile, this old woman looks like she might keel over at any second. Where the hell is that kid's parent?

The bus doors close. As the driver shifts into gear and the bus lurches forward, the bent old lady sprawls backward. The way she leans reminds Tamara of someone cocking the hammer of a pistol. Fortunately, a young man seated nearby notices and catches her. Just as he stands to offer his seat, the little boy leaps down. The old woman thanks the man for helping but waves him off, saying it will be easier if she's nearer the door.

Tamara's phone says it's already half past ten. This commute is becoming a serious thorn in her side. More than an hour on the bus each way, plus the twenty-minute walks from home to bus stop, shop to bus stop, all for a wage barely above minimum. What's the point? It's not a livable income. She'll never pay off her debts this way. Never be able to afford a place of her own. Her life is going nowhere, but she's stuck on this godforsaken bus day after day.

Great. And now her phone is frozen on the home screen. She can't even numb her

(pain)

brain with senseless memes and fake news and photos of other people's trips to Santorini.

She shuts her eyes and leans back, her head bouncing against the rear wall. She always prefers to sit in the back if she can. Today, she's got the center seat, perched over the aisle like a queen on her throne. The engine vibrates underneath, giving rise to a not altogether unpleasant ticklish sensation between her legs. The bus, like all the other buses on this route, is old and broken down, spotted with rust and caked with years of exhaust fumes. The seats are stained, chipped, burnt, scarred. A rank, stale odor hangs in the air. It has probably been pounding the concrete as long as Tamara has been alive, no money in the city budget for upgrades.

Tamara lifts her phone, taps the screen a few times. Nothing happens. When she drops her hand in frustration, her breath hitches.

That boy is standing right in front of her. Staring at her.

Startled by the little creep, she holds back a shriek but can't stop her right elbow from reflexively jerking to the side. It jabs into the man sitting beside her. Right into his funny bone, it seems, because he sucks a harsh breath through his teeth, rubs his arm vigorously, and sends an angry, offended glare Tamara's way.

The kid's not dancing anymore. He's just standing there, an idiotic smile on his lips as he peers at her without blinking. She stares back, unsettled by his proximity. What the hell does he think he's doing? Having a staring contest? She thinks about shouting *Boo!* to spook him, or else offering a few muttered curse words to shoo him away, but for all she knows, the parent is sitting nearby. The last thing she needs right now is an argument with some disgruntled single mom or deadbeat dad.

Tamara looks to either side. No one else is paying the boy any attention. She leans forward.

"Where's your, uh...guardian?"

Now that she's looking at him up close, she can see how grimy he is. He doesn't smell too bad, but his clothes are tattered and torn, long streaks of dirt blended into the fabric. His hair is greasy and matted. A fat lip, a bruised eye. Is that a dried streak of blood dripping down his brow?

"Hey, are you...okay?"

Finally, he reacts. He lifts his right hand. Tamara gasps at the sight of it. It's swollen and totally discolored—purple and yellow and red—and it hangs from his wrist at an abnormal angle. Like the bones are shattered.

He holds out his hand, a sneaky look in his squinty eyes. For a moment, Tamara thinks he's about to flip her off. Then, slowly, he uncurls his fingers to show her.

Tamara squirms with discomfort.

It's a tooth.

A big, front tooth with no roots. Broken off, the thick end jagged and sharp-edged.

The boy spreads his lips in a smile, revealing a gap right in front. The left central incisor is missing except for a tiny, sharp nub jutting from his gums. A drop of blood falls onto his lower teeth, and he licks it away before shutting his mouth.

Tamara begins to panic. She's about to stand up and demand that the kid's parent come forward, about to plead to the general decency of all these oblivious riders, but the boy stops her. He somehow wedges himself right between her legs, leans close to her ear, and whispers.

"For the Tooth Fairy."

Without waiting for a response, he turns and scampers up the aisle toward the front of the bus.

Tamara, her mouth hanging open, appeals silently to the passengers on either side of her. The man to her right gives a guarded glance and scoots away. The couple to her left are too busy canoodling to have noticed anything, but the girl sees Tamara peering at them and returns a spiteful glare.

The bus slows to a much smoother halt at the next stop. Air bursts from the pneumatic pistons as the doors fold open. Nobody gets off, and the driver curses at whoever pushed the button. No one gets on either, so the driver shifts into gear before the doors are even closed. A young, wide-eyed man suddenly springs forward, waving his arms and calling out to the driver. "Stop! Stop!"

The driver slams on the brakes, barking profanely at the passenger. Nervously, the man apologizes and tries to explain that he was reading and it won't happen again but he'll be late if he misses his stop. The little boy is standing right beside the driver, staring up at him with something like awe, not at all shocked by the filthy language, but almost reverent. The driver opens the door, telling the man in colorful words that he's no longer welcome on this bus.

As the bus merges into traffic, Tamara sees the little boy fiddling with something near the front. It looks like he's reaching for the driver's controls. She realizes he's got his arm shoved deep into the farebox. All the way. Up to the shoulder. A smug grin plastered across his face. He's looking right at Tamara as he pulls his arm out, clutching a wad of singles.

Tamara isn't sure what happens next. It happens too quickly, too disjointedly.

It feels as though the bus hits a pothole. At the same time, the boy—Billy Clepto, Tamara has just decided to name him —poses as if to sprint down the aisle, straight at Tamara. She doesn't actually see him run, or see him at all; he's suddenly a blur, a missile launched at her face. A shock rumbles through her body, everything pulsing and quaking like being paddled by a defibrillator. The boy's face has been transported from the front of the bus to mere inches from her nose. It blocks out everything else. All she sees is his filthy, bruised, and scraped visage, his broken tooth, his unblinking eyes. But his flesh looks different. Yellowish-gray. His eyes are rolled back, his brow folded in a wicked, hateful frown, his nostrils flared obnoxiously wide. Veins bulge at his temples as his jaw opens wider than humanly possible, revealing a cavernous brown throat with dripping, rippling walls—

And then, just like that, he's gone.

Tamara doesn't even have time to gasp or wince or swear.

Did she imagine it?

She must have. That stupid job and this stupid commute have whittled away at what little brain matter she has, and it's taking a toll. She really needs to consider quitting. She can find something else. Closer to home. Maybe even something that pays better. After all, she doesn't owe anything to her lecherous boss. She gets along with her coworkers just fine, but she doesn't really like any of them.

At times like this, when she actually allows herself to think about it, it seems so easy. *Just quit. Walk out. Then everything will be better.* Yeah, well, if it's so goddamn easy, then why hasn't she done it yet?

The answer's simple enough. It's because she—

What the hell?

Where did this money come from?

Tamara stares stupidly at her hands. In her left, her phone, still frozen on the home screen. In her right, a crumpled handful of bills. Singles.

Though it's not even warm in the bus, sweat plunges down

her brow. Her heart bumps and thumps in sync with the wheels bouncing over cracks in the road.

Where's Billy Clepto? And how did he deposit these stolen bills in her hand?

She scans the bus. At first, she doesn't see him. Then—

"*Aah!*"

She pipes out a short, high-pitched squeal when he pops up in the next row like a jack-in-the-box. He's in the window seat the young man vacated at the last stop, facing backward and staring directly at Tamara.

Her neighbors flinch when she screams, each of them castigating her with dirty looks.

Billy Clepto has turned his attention to the couple beside Tamara. The guy's arm is wrapped around the girl, his face buried in the crook of her neck. The girl's head is thrown back, eyes closed, legs crossed so her skirt rides high up her thighs. She's giggling softly as his tongue tickles her earlobe, and his right hand is in his pocket. It looks like he's diddling himself while he makes out with her. Grossed out but unable to peel her eyes away, Tamara slides over and bumps into the man on her right.

"Watch it," the man grumbles.

A mischievous glimmer glints in Billy Clepto's eyes.

He grins at Tamara, flashing the sharpened nub of a tooth, then reaches over the chairback. Leaning forward, he places his hand on the woman's thigh. Rubbing, squeezing, inching slowly up her leg.

Tamara gapes in shock. She wants to say something but can hardly believe that a boy so young would ever consciously violate a woman like this. The girl squirms delightedly in her seat, apparently under the impression that it's her boyfriend's hand.

Suddenly, the young boy rams his hand underneath her skirt.

The girl goes rigid and slaps her boyfriend, cursing him out with venomous whispers, reminding him that they're in public. The angry spat brings an abrupt end to their PDA, and the woman resorts to staring out the window. She never even notices Billy Clepto, who was quick to turn around and face forward before she saw his groping paw.

Repulsed by what she's just witnessed, Tamara leans over to tell the couple what happened, rat the little pervert out. They both sneer and turn away, refusing even to make eye contact.

As the bus wheels up to the next stop, Billy Clepto is nowhere to be seen.

Someone taps the tip of Tamara's sneaker. She looks down. The little boy is on all fours in the aisle, grinning inanely. Before she can make sense of what he's doing down there, the middle-aged man in the seat beside him springs up on his way to the exit. He trips over Billy Clepto and sprawls face-first into the aisle. A few friendly hands help him up. He stares around frantically, blood pouring from both nostrils, and then hastily makes his way off the bus.

No one gets on.

Billy Clepto is hiding underneath the two vacated seats. Once again, none of the other passengers have noticed his cruel prank.

Before the next stop, which is only three blocks away, Billy Clepto reaches across the aisle into a businessman's suit pocket. He removes the man's wallet and hides it under the seat. As the bus pulls up to the stop, the man goes for his traffic card and realizes his wallet is missing. The driver refuses to wait for him, and the man becomes irate when he misses his stop. He curses out the driver and yells at those seated around him, accusing them of being pickpockets until somebody points out the wallet at his feet. When he exits at the following stop, he slams his hand against the door so hard that a hairline crack appears in the glass.

After that, Billy Clepto spends some more time crouched on the floor. Tamara can't tell what he's doing. She is still trying to identify the kid's parent, and she's distracted, constantly thanking her lucky stars that she has not been as promiscuous as some of her friends or her cousin, Gloria. Better to wallow in her shitty job, shitty commute, and shitty living situation with her folks than to be responsible for a little devil like Billy Clepto. She does not have the patience for this unhinged behavior, nor can she understand how any parent puts up with it.

So, that's what he was doing.

Billy Clepto has stood up. His hands are cupped before him, filled with black, filthy dust bunnies, flecks of mud, and crumbs. He steps into the empty row, stands on his tiptoes, and sprinkles the detritus into the hair of the two passengers in the next row up. It's a teenage boy with long hair tied in a bun and an older woman with a much larger bun of gray hair. Neither one feels the scraps landing on their heads, but it's not long before tainted snowflakes of dust and dirt fall into their laps. The woman immediately stands up and jabs the button for a stop. The teenager glances around with a bemused smirk. As he brushes the filth from his hair, he makes eye contact with Tamara, giving her an unreadable expression. Then, he shrugs and cracks open the window beside him.

Same as before, no one seems to have noticed Billy's antics.

"Hey," whispers Tamara. She gets up and moves into the empty row, trapping Billy Clepto in the window seat. "Where's your mom?"

The boy stares at her. When the bus starts moving, he stands up on the seat and starts doing his worm dance again. Seeing it so close, Tamara shivers with revulsion. There's something unnatural about the way the boy moves, like his bones are made of rubber. She doesn't want to touch the urchin, so she just repeats her question. This time, Billy points at her.

"Uh! I'm not..." Tamara crosses her arms and turns away. She is about to return to her center seat in the back row, but someone has taken it. A middle-aged, curmudgeonly man with Coke-bottle spectacles. He must have gotten on at the last stop. No other empty seats remain, so it's either sit next to this little creep or stand in the aisle.

Tamara puffs out her chest and huffs an irritated breath, glancing side-eyed at the boy.

"What the fu...?" she mutters, trailing off in utter disbelief.

Billy Clepto is clinging to the window like a gecko.

The couple behind Tamara is bickering. The bus has hit a patch of open road, so the driver punches the accelerator. Tamara's head jerks backward. Someone up front drops some-thing. The boy scrambles higher, onto the ceiling. He crawls around in a circle like a dog chasing its tail. The bus seems to be driving much too fast for a city street. Tamara feels like she's getting motion sickness, but she can't take her eyes off the boy above her. How is he doing that? Why doesn't anyone else see him?

As they approach a red light, the driver hits the brakes, tires squealing on the pavement. Tamara's head is flung forward so fast that her face slams into the chairback in front of her. Right in the eye. Shit. If she has a black eye, her mother's going to want to know what happened. Her boss won't let her work the register. She'll be relegated to unloading and organizing shipments in the back for a week. Again.

All around her, people are shifting in their seats, but Billy Clepto seems to be having a grand old time. He's smiling and messing around with the emergency escape hatch. Unexpectedly, he disengages from the ceiling and drops down on the other side of the aisle. He lands in the lap of a woman seated by the window, one row ahead of Tamara. She must be the boy's mother. Billy is looking at her, trying to get her attention, but she only stares out the window. When he wiggles his fingers near her cheek, tickling her, the woman itches her face but still doesn't acknowledge him.

What a shitty mother. That, Tamara realizes, is exactly the sort of mother she would be if she ever got herself knocked up.

The man sitting beside the woman removes a bottle of Mountain Dew from his satchel. The colorful liquid draws Billy Clepto's attention. The boy stares greedily as the man unscrews the top and lifts the bottle to his mouth.

Just as the man tilts his head back, Billy slaps the bottle. Neon soda spills down the man's chin and shirt, spraying as the bottle falls to the floor. A few drops land on Tamara's sneakers. A puddle of carbonated piss forms in the aisle. The man gapes at his hands in surprise. Billy Clepto titters silently beside him, but the man doesn't even look at him.

The driver must have seen it happen in the rearview mirror. They're still at the red light, and he stands up, sticking his head out of his cubby.

"Hey, you! You'd better clean that up!"

The light changes. Cars start moving around them. Horns blare from behind.

"How'm I gonna clean it up? With what?"

"I don't give a shit! The shirt on your back for all I care! Shouldn't be drinking on my goddamn bus!"

The man gazes around at his neighbors. No one speaks up in his defense. Not even Tamara, who saw the little delinquent do it.

"Sorry, I don't have a cleaning kit with me!" the man yells back at the driver.

A chorus of horns blares outside.

"Then you're off!" bellows the driver. He opens the exit doors. "Off the bus! Now!"

"This isn't a bus stop! We're in the middle of traffic!"

"I don't give a good goddamn! Get off or I throw you off!"

The man grabs his satchel and rushes out. More horns blare as traffic is stopped by a pedestrian in the middle of the street. The yellow liquid has begun to run forward, and when the driver punches the gas, it reverses direction, running toward the back.

Tamara glares at the boy responsible for this. If no one puts a stop to his mischief, it's going to take her all night to get home.

Now that the man's seat is empty, Tamara can get a better look. She leans forward, trying to see the boy's mother's face.

How can she ignore her son when he's sitting right on her lap?

Tamara gasps.

The boy is not sitting on her lap. At a glance, it would look like he's standing between her legs. But Tamara can see clearly that the woman's legs are crossed.

Billy Clepto is standing *through* her legs.

Suddenly, the boy notices Tamara looking. He comes toward her, and Tamara gasps again as he steps, not around the empty seat, but *through* it. Just like before, he holds out his dirty hand. This time, there are two broken teeth.

"For the Tooth Fairy." He winks. His smile now reveals a wide gap, front and center, with two pointed nubs.

Tamara barely notices. She's still wondering how the kid walked through the chair.

"Are...are..." she stutters. Her mind knows what she wants to ask, but the words won't come out. "Are you..." This is crazy. Maybe she fell asleep. She's dreaming this madness. There's no other explanation. "Are you...a ghost?"

The words don't even sound real. Who actually finds themself in a position to ask such a thing?

Rather than answering, the boy looks down at the now-empty bottle of Mountain Dew. He kicks it, and it rattles and bounces along the floor toward the front of the bus. Passengers watch it roll past. The driver barks a fresh curse word, but when people glance back, they don't seem to notice Billy. Instead, they appear to be glaring at Tamara.

Billy Clepto saunters up the aisle. A woman sitting near the exit doors has dozed off with her purse resting on her knees. Hooking his finger under the shoulder strap, the boy gives a strong tug. The purse falls into the aisle. Bits and pieces of this woman's private life tumble into the sticky yellow puddle. The woman wakes with a start, sees her effects sprawled below, and immediately begins crying. Her neighbors help to retrieve the spilled items as they roll away under the bus's momentum. The driver swerves into the right-hand lane, pumping the brakes as they approach the next stop.

The little old lady is having trouble getting to her feet. With everyone helping pick up the younger woman's things, nobody notices the elder's difficulty. Nobody except Billy Clepto.

Tamara is shaking her head. She's trying to get the old woman's attention as Billy steps up to her. She's just about to cry out to alert someone, anyone, everyone, so certain is she that the boy's hijinks will cause irreparable harm to the frail woman.

However, all Billy does is support the old woman's elbow. He eases her out of the seat and escorts her the few steps to the exit. He even helps adjust the strap on her tote bag so it doesn't slip off her shoulder. He guides her all the way out, holding her hand until she is safely clear of the bus.

Maybe the little hellion isn't so bad after all.

The others finally get the young woman's purse sorted out. They retake their seats, all of them wiping their hands on pant legs and shirt sleeves because now they are covered in sticky soda. Billy presses the stop request button and then goes around tickling people, blowing in hair and faces, untucking shirts and unbuttoning buttons—all fairly harmless stunts that leave Tamara feeling much better about the remainder of this bus ride. She even catches herself giggling a few times after seeing people's reactions to Billy's tricks.

At the next stop, no one stands up. The driver swears

savagely, warning the passengers not to touch the button unless they mean to get off. As soon as the bus lurches into traffic, Billy pushes the button again. This pattern continues for the next two stops, goading the driver into a volcanic rage, and Tamara can no longer stop herself from laughing out loud.

She hasn't laughed in days. Weeks, maybe. All at once, she finds herself gazing at the crumpled dollar bills in her fist with gratitude. Billy Clepto is doing his dance again, and she looks at him with endearment, silently thanking him for providing this moment of reprieve from her monotonous, stressful, dead-end life. She thinks about how nice it would be to have someone like that around all the time. Not a child, necessarily, but someone with whom she can be silly and goof around. She's already forgotten the ridiculous notion that the boy might be a ghost. As he performs his wriggling dance, she only passingly notices how his feet are hovering six inches off the ground.

Three noisy, rough-looking youths board the bus. They stomp down the aisle, and Billy does not step aside. They walk right through him, never noticing his presence, but the boy has reached into one of their pockets and removed a small, rectangular object. It glints in the glare of a passing streetlight. The three teens spread out in the vacated seats near the back, surrounding Tamara. Once they realize they've stepped in spilled soda, they all start swearing with some of the foulest language Tamara has ever heard.

Billy stands near the exit door. There's a soft *clinking* sound. Then a spark. A flame. Soon, the smell of burning plastic fills the bus.

While the passengers glance around with concern, Billy

Clepto brings his new toy over to a man wearing flip-flops. The flame rises from the Zippo, and Billy bends over, setting it down near the man's toes.

Tamara looks around at the teens, trying to remember which one Billy took it from. She taps the scariest of the bunch on the shoulder.

"Is that your lighter?" she says, pointing at the flame on the floor.

"What?" sneers the teen, flashing stained teeth.

The man in flip-flops leaps screaming from his chair.

Tamara points again at the flame. "That! There! Is that yours?"

"Oh, shit!"

The teen dashes forward, stumbling between seats as the bus makes a wide right turn. He grabs his lighter, flicks it closed, and stares at it in bewilderment before returning to his friends. The man in flip-flops examines his blistered toes and moves to a different seat. The three teens are huddled over the Zippo, flicking it, discussing how it could have possibly fallen and lit itself.

Stunned passengers cover their noses and crack windows to dilute the scent of burnt plastic and scorched flesh. Billy Clepto has approached a woman seated near the middle of the bus, just in front of the exit doors. She's busily typing on her phone. Seeing this, Tamara remembers her own phone and, forgetting it's frozen, attempts to open the camera app. She shoves the crumpled singles into her jacket pocket, taps furiously at the screen, swearing when nothing happens. Her phone is so old that she really shouldn't be surprised, but there's just no way she can afford a new one. If the phone is dead, this commute to and from work is going to be unbearable. At least Billy is here to distract her tonight. But what about tomorrow? And the next day?

A scream rises from up front. The woman who was glued to her phone has stood up. She's complaining about something, holding the back of her neck, and pointing at her seat. On top of the chairback, a sharp flap of metal has come loose. It's bent, pointing treacherously upward directly where someone might place their neck. She becomes hysterical when she sees that her palm is painted red. Blood drips to the floor. A steady stream runs between her shoulder blades, soaking into the back of her blouse.

Billy Clepto guffaws with laughter, but no sound escapes his mouth. At this distance, it's hard to tell, but Tamara thinks that he's lost more teeth since he last showed her. She shivers at the thought and runs her tongue around her mouth to confirm her own dental integrity.

An elderly man has offered the bleeding woman his handkerchief. She's holding it to her neck, crying, and pleading with the driver to let her off. Billy has moved over to the emergency exit window. He's fiddling with the handle, like he's trying to open it while the bus is in motion, but he's pushing it in the wrong direction.

Snap!

The handle breaks off. Billy lets it clatter to the floor. No one notices over the sound of the bloodied woman's cries.

Finally, they come to the next bus stop. The driver stomps on the brakes. Everyone on board is thrown forward. Several people bash their heads on the seats in front of them. The bus is parked askew beside the curb. The bleeding woman's cries grow louder as she runs out, still cursing the bus driver from the sidewalk. A young man boards the bus and notices the driver's livid expression, the passengers' stunned faces, the general air of disquiet. Even though he already deposited his fare, he retreats, mumbling that he'll catch the next one.

Tamara's lip is bleeding. That last skidding stop hurled her mouth into the chairback. The taste of blood makes her sick. She runs her tongue along her teeth again, afraid she might have chipped one.

Billy Clepto's pranks have taken a dark turn that Tamara doesn't like. All she wants is to be home so she can burrow into bed and forget all of this. Maybe this is exactly what she needs. She imagines herself waking up late tomorrow, calling in sick to work—no, calling in to quit—and then, finally, once and for all, making some decisions to put her life in order. She'll find a new job closer to home, with better hours and better pay. She'll reconnect with friends she hasn't seen in a while. She'll start taking her parents' advice. Maybe she'll even reach out to Gloria and get to know her cousin's kids. They can't possibly be as bad as this.

Billy resumes his dance and coughs up a mouthful of blood with a few more fractured teeth. His flesh is pasty and bruised, the look in his eyes diabolical, and his smile just a series of sharp, broken nubs. No one else sees him. Tamara remembers that he's, what? A ghost? Is he even real? Or just a figment of her imagination? He could be a hallucination induced by stress. Unless—

Oh, no.

Has she forgotten to take her medication?

The last time she forgot, she injured a customer. Her bosses knew about her condition, and they were very understanding, but that was why she'd been transferred to a different location on the other end of the city. They had been willing to put their necks on the line for her, give her a second chance. What other employer would do that for someone like Tamara? She wouldn't be able to find another job, and without this job, what would she have?

Once, she intentionally skipped a few doses, which led to her trying to seduce her best friend's fiancé, believing he wanted her and that her bestie was involved in a cultish conspiracy against her. She lost most of her friends after that mix-up. Another time, she caused an uproar at the family Christmas party when she unleashed a vicious tirade of unrepeatable language at Gloria and her husband, then slapped one of their kids. Since then, she's no longer allowed at family functions.

And Tamara is certain that her parents loathe her. They allow her to stay and even try to help. Daily reminders to take her meds, one of them always around to keep an eye on her. But do they *like* her? Do they *want* the burden of a mental case daughter in their lives? Of course not. No more than Tamara wants a child of her own, like that time she—

No!

She is not supposed to think about that.

Tamara is vaguely aware that Billy Clepto is messing around with the exit doors, but she's not paying attention. She stares stubbornly ahead, lost in thought, striving to push that one awful memory down because she knows what it does to her. Instead, she's tracing her steps back through the day, trying to remember whether or not she's taken her pills. She always takes them after lunch, but today...she can't remember. How can she when every day is exactly the same? She took them yesterday and the day before and the day before that, so why wouldn't she have taken them today?

Billy's fingers are pinched between the exit doors. He's trying to pry them apart. No one realizes what's happening, but as the crack widens, the draft flowing through the bus gets stronger.

Maybe Tamara should not be dredging up past mistakes but trying to stop this little gremlin. Billy Clepto. This supposed hallucination in the midst of terrorizing a busful of innocent people. But Tamara can't help herself thinking backward, and she doesn't recall a single instance—before or after the diagnosis—when she suffered from hallucinations. Voices and intrusive thoughts, sure, all the time. But visual hallucinations? When has she ever seen something or someone that wasn't there?

But then, how would she know whether something is real or not?

The pneumatic pistons release an unexpected burst of condensed air as the exit doors are wrenched apart. The bus is barreling down the road. Wind blasts inside. At least two hats are torn from heads and launched toward the rear of the bus. The brim of one catches a man in the eye. The people seated near the doors are screaming. The driver stares and shouts at his rearview. When he realizes what has happened, he hauls on the lever for the exit doors. Nothing happens. An old man falls out of his seat, tumbling toward the gaping hole as cars speed past outside.

Tamara searches for Billy. She stands up and finally sees him crouched low to the ground, slowly pushing the old man toward the exit. Just before the man falls out, the driver swerves into the right lane and slams on the brakes. He stomps out of his booth, charging at the exit doors. Passengers help to haul the old man back inside.

Before the driver arrives, Billy pushes the doors closed.

There's a brief, heated discussion among the alarmed passengers and the driver. After checking the mechanisms and controls, the driver determines there's nothing seriously wrong with the doors. Must have been a fluke. He'll have the mechanics look at it tonight, but this is the end of his shift, and he intends to finish it. If anyone has a problem with that, they can get off and fend for themselves.

Two or three people grab their things. Billy Clepto trips the last one. The girl face plants onto the concrete outside, and the driver pulls away without checking on her.

Everyone on the bus looks on edge now. No one is dozing or staring absently out the windows. Tamara wonders whether she should have gotten off with the others. In the heat of the moment, she hadn't even considered it. She'd been too busy watching Billy as he wandered over to the young girl with too much makeup. Tamara thinks Billy will start groping her like he did the girl in back. Instead, he shoves his hand into her stomach—right through her shirt and belly button, buried in her guts—and winds it like twisting a faucet handle. The girl still hasn't noticed, although her face grows pale. She looks like she'll be sick. Just seeing her makes Tamara's stomach turn over.

Gleefully, Billy Clepto snatches his hand back. The girl immediately leans forward, her eyes wide as she vomits on the floor between her knees. Billy leaps out of the way. The passengers nearby vacate, scrambling to avoid the splatter and claim new seats. The driver is shouting again. *"What the hell happened this time?"* The nauseating smell filters throughout the bus. People are opening windows and stabbing the stop request button, just about everyone ready to get off now.

Tamara peers outside, trying to identify where they are exactly. They're passing the library, which means it's ten more stops until hers. Too far to walk unless she plans to get home after midnight.

But why not? She's a grown woman. She can come home late if she wants.

Sure she can, if she wants her folks to phone the police, assuming their daughter forgot to take her meds and went off the rails again.

Maybe she ought to play it safe and just take a dose right now. She'll have to swallow them dry, but if she did forget this afternoon, she'll only continue to spiral the longer she waits. She reaches into her pocket, wading through the crumpled bills for the vial. As she pulls it out, she vaguely wonders how Billy—being a ghost or a hallucination or whatever he is—could have given her a handful of real money. No answer comes to her, and she shrugs it off, popping the cap and preparing two pills. She waits for a buildup of saliva, then gulps them down, wincing as the pills slowly tunnel through her esophagus.

Tamara closes her eyes, focuses on the rumbling engine, the bumps in the road. After allowing time for the pills to complete the journey and begin dissolving in her stomach, she takes a deep breath and opens her eyes, fully expecting Billy Clepto to have vanished.

But Billy is right there, staring intently at the little hammer meant for breaking windows in an emergency. His hips are still swiveling, but almost imperceptibly. What does that even mean? Everything he does is imperceptible to everyone except Tamara.

"Hey, you little shit!" she blurts out.

All the passengers turn to glare at her. Billy doesn't even look up. He's too busy cocking his arm back, pretending to swing a hammer to pound nails or windows or skulls. He steps back into the aisle, swinging his arm in a way that looks obscene performed by the little boy's body. Too much force for such a small thing. He looks like a major league pitcher or a firefighter swinging an axe, but trapped in a shrunken shell. Billy creeps toward the driver's cubby, practicing his violent, empty-handed swings with each step, occasionally pausing to poke a mystified passenger.

Finally, he reaches the front, cocks his elbow back, and takes an unsettlingly realistic practice swing right into the driver's booth.

All at once, Tamara understands what's coming.

Her brain is telling her a hundred things at once. Like usual, she is unsure whether to believe the messages. Her mind has never been her most reliable asset. Especially if she forgot to take her meds. The pills she just took might not kick in for another twenty minutes.

With a determined sneer, Billy returns from the driver's booth, stalking down the aisle like a predator with his mouthful of tiny razor teeth, glowering at the ignorant passengers all around him, none of whom have any idea that he's been the cause of this hellish bus ride or that it's about to get a whole lot worse. He returns to the emergency hammer and grasps the handle, preparing to rip it from its holster.

"Leave that alone!" yells Tamara, standing up and lurching with the bus's motion. The other passengers go rigid, gaping at Tamara's outburst. "Whose kid is that? Where's the parent? Take control of your fucking child!" She's stomping toward the center of the bus, screaming into strangers' faces. "He's going to get us all killed!"

"What the hell's going on back there?" shouts the driver. "You! You there! Sit down or I swear on my mother I'll toss you out!"

The emergency hammer snaps loose and clatters to the floor. No one hears it; no one notices. They're all too engrossed in this newest disturbance.

But Tamara sees it. And she sees Billy Clepto pick it up, cock his arm back in the same manner he was practicing, and race toward the front of the bus.

"Stop it!" screeches Tamara. "Put it down! Someone stop him!"

Voices mutter all around her.

"Who's she talking to?"

"Where'd she get that?"

"I hate this fucking route."

"I told you to take a seat, lady!" screams the irate driver, his furious eyes blazing at her through the rearview.

Billy is too fast. He reaches the driver's booth before Tamara, and he's already swinging at the driver's arms with the hammer. Tamara lunges just in time, grabbing the boy and knocking the hammer from his hand. It flies forward, cracking the windshield before clattering near the entry door.

"You crazy bitch!" barks the driver. "You'll be arrested for thi—*MOTHERFU*—"

He stomps on the brakes. Passengers are thrown from their seats. People wail with terror and shock.

And Tamara, standing next to the driver's booth, looks up, dumbfounded to see that Billy Clepto is not in her arms.

He's outside. In the crosswalk. A backpack hanging from one shoulder.

The boy stares in horror at the behemoth bearing down on him. His wide eyes are fixed on Tamara, his mouth pried open, his hands held up as though to shield himself from a stray ball.

The last thing Tamara notices before she crashes through the windshield is Billy's teeth in the glare of the bus's headlights. They're all there, in his mouth, sparkly and straight and unbroken.

Glass explodes around Tamara, chewing into her face and arms. She hears the sickening crunch of the bus striking a body and is vaguely aware of a small, limp form being flung through the air beside her. She blacks out when her head hits the pavement.

Before Tamara dies, she's woken by something nudging against her belly. Her eyes struggle to open. She can't breathe because her lungs have been punctured by her broken ribs. Pain rages all over her body. It feels like every bone is splintered, every organ pulverized. But she senses something moving against her side.

With immense effort, screaming in silent agony, she looks down and sees the boy, Billy Clepto, curled into her lap. He's gazing into her face, tears pouring from his eyes, bruises and scrapes disfiguring his innocent flesh. All of his teeth are shattered, leaving only tiny, sharp nubs. He's grasping on to Tamara's midsection, pleading for help, asking *Why, why, why?*

Tamara wants to hug him, but she can't move any part of her body. She tries to say *I'm sorry*. No words come out, only a gurgle of blood and saliva. After a moment, she realizes her jawbone has been torn off.

Then, she remembers.

She did take her meds. After lunch. Just like every other day.

At least she won't have to worry about forgetting anymore. And she'll never have to ride that godforsaken bus again.

Trembling from pain and an unendurable terror of the unknown, Billy Clepto dies staring into Tamara's bloodshot eyes. Soon after, before the paramedics arrive to separate them, Tamara follows the boy, willingly.

The Hogs of Aie Valley

"Let's check out this road."

"Where does it go?"

"Don't know." Tae-wook peers ahead. Their dog, an over-grown black Jindo named Hobbes, pulls at the leash. "All the more reason to explore. Get to know your surroundings."

"We're not on a military campaign, Tae," Eliza scoffs as she takes out her phone. She opens the map app, zooms in on their location. "It doesn't go anywhere. Dead end."

"There must be something there. Hobbes is going nuts. Come on."

Tae-wook and Eliza have lived in the village for two weeks now. The first two years of their marriage they spent in a tiny one-bedroom in Seoul, which was fine until they adopted Hobbes. The dog was small, and they never imagined he would grow as big as he has. Even as a puppy, Hobbes was generally well-mannered, though somewhat skittish and terri-torial. Certain sounds from the street or neighboring apartments agitated his wolfish inclinations, summoning long, melancholy howls. When strangers came to the door, he produced a low growl like an idling motorcycle. Once, when a woman from the district office stopped by to check for gas leaks, Hobbes frightened her off before she could begin.

With their work, moving away from the city was a feasible option. Sure, they would be farther from friends and conveniences, but it's not like they were moving to the remote countryside.

Aie Valley—pronounced like *eye* and meaning *child* in Korean—is a small village sheltered by modest mountains, about fifteen minutes northwest of Seoul. They found a sensibly priced condo with plenty of room for the three of them and secured the down payment with help from Tae-wook's rich aunt. The benefits for Hobbes were evident immediately. The mountain trails provided better walks than Seoul's chaotic city streets. There were plenty of open spaces where Hobbes could run, and he was finally able to sleep through the night.

During these first two weeks, they have been out with Hobbes every day, so they've already learned that Aie Valley differs from your typical village. Not in a bad way, but definitely unlike any place either of them has ever lived. It is one of the few villages in modern-day Korea that still uses *jangse-ungs*, wooden totem poles erected at village boundaries to ward off evil spirits. There are several mysterious, abandoned buildings. Some of the locals are overly friendly, others are standoffish, and a few are downright creepy. Nestled in the mountains, the valley is prone to heavy fogs and drastic temperature changes. Many of the locals maintain small farm plots; the amount and variety of scarecrows is laughable.

Speaking of the crows, they are noisier than city crows, constantly *kyawing* back and forth, and yet they don't seem to bother Hobbes at all. He just watches them, whereas the birds in the city sent him off like a banshee. Also, Eliza swears she has heard the birds pronounce human words in both Korean and English. Along the mountain trails can be found several wartime bunkers, and there is a village resident—an old man with no hands—who claims there is unexploded ordinance from the Korean War scattered all throughout the valley. Some delivery drivers refuse to enter the village, some wildlife residing in the mountains apparently cannot be found in any other part of the country, and every single valley resident they've spoken with has asked them if they've seen the ghosts yet. Plural. *Ghosts.*

The road they've just turned onto is not so much a road as a wide, paved walkway. A car could squeeze along the lane if it had to, but if two cars met coming in opposite directions, one would be forced to back out. To the left is a largish garden planted with rows of vegetables, and to the right, an empty plot that was probably once a garden. Now, it's just hard-packed earth, overgrown with weeds and decorated by heaps of trash. Low-rising, rusted iron fences run along either side of the road, though gaping holes render them virtually useless.

Hobbes has gone ahead, pulling the leash taut. Soon, the fences end, replaced by trees and underbrush encroaching on both sides. Branches hang over their heads, leaving only a narrow strip of blue visible above. At their feet, sprawling bushes, vines, and weeds creep onto the blacktop.

"This is claustrophobic," comments Eliza.

"It's no different from the trails we usually walk."

"It feels different."

Tae-wook shrugs and points at Hobbes. "Someone likes it, though. Look at him go."

"Hobbes!" Eliza calls. The dog stops and glances back. When neither of them gives further instructions, he takes off at a run.

"Oww!" squeaks Tae-wook. "He almost pulled my arm out of its socket."

The road continues at a slight incline. It grows narrower as the branches meet overhead, completing the tunnel effect and consuming them in shade. Eventually, the trees above open up again, spraying them with what remains of the daylight. The underbrush backs off as well. Both Tae-wook and Eliza breathe sighs of relief. Hobbes, though still drawn forward by some instinctual compulsion, finally slows to their pace. He gives the leash some slack and walks just in front of his owners. Now, they're all enjoying the walk. Tae-wook keeps his eyes peeled for birds, Eliza hums a new melody she's been working on, and Hobbes sniffs eagerly at the fresh mountain air.

Ahead, they see a tall iron fence. Behind it, a structure.

Tae-wook pauses. Eliza and Hobbes tug at his arms, turning to stare with wonder when they feel his resistance.

"Tae? What's wrong?"

"Nothing. I just... Something doesn't feel right."

Eliza giggles and tugs harder. Seeing that someone lives down this road makes her feel a lot better.

Tae-wook remains unmoving. "This might be...private property. Might belong to one of those, uh...village freaks."

"Freaks?!" Eliza peals with laughter.

"Shhh!"

"Hey, you're the one who wanted to explore. We're here, so we might as well have a look."

The closer they come, the less nervous Tae-wook feels. It's a perfectly regular property. Both the fence and the house are old but in decent condition. The fence gate is wide open, almost welcoming them in. They stop before they reach it, exchanging glances. Hobbes wanders off the road to sniff the forest floor. The sign hung beside the gate reads *Aie Valley Pension*.

The building seems out of place. Built in a Western style, it resembles a Victorian mansion. This, in a way, puts Eliza even more at ease. The neighborhood where she grew up contained several such houses, though most were a hundred years old and in violent states of disrepair. This one appears rather well cared for, though it's a bit weatherworn and sports a chaotic tangle of vines around the upper floors. There are no vehicles in the expansive gravel lot, no one hanging around on the porch, the grounds, or the garden off to the right. It's one of those places, similar to remote Buddhist temples, that perpetually feel like no one has been there in ages.

A separate building—two-storied, long, narrow—stands at the rear of the property, mostly hidden behind the main structure. It looks like servants' quarters or a budget motel. Since this is a pension, those must be the smaller, cheaper rooms. The main house is most likely segregated by floor, with larger rentals intended for groups or families. Presumably, this was once a desirable base for hikers wishing to immerse themselves in the mountainous landscape.

They walk right up to the open gate, stopping where the blacktop ends and the gravel lot begins. Tae-wook hands the leash to Eliza, who is peering curiously into the grounds.

Hobbes stops sniffing and sits, gazing into the property with as much interest as Eliza. Tae-wook scrolls through his phone.

"What are you doing?" asks Eliza.

"Here it is. The pension has a listing on Naver. There's a phone number. Should I?"

Eliza shrugs. "Sure."

Tae-wook dials and puts it on speakerphone. It rings and rings, and he's just about to hang up when a woman answers.

"*Yes?*"

"Hi," responds Tae-wook, surprised. "Uh...is this the owner of the Aie Valley Pension?"

"*How did you...? No, not exactly.*"

"Oh, uh..."

"*My family moved off that property years ago.*"

"I see. It's just that this is the number listed on Naver."

"*My brother's a lazy asshole. He should have taken that down.*"

"Do you happen to know who the current owners are?"

"*I didn't even know the place was still standing. Are you looking to... How did you find out about it?*"

"We just moved to the village. Out for a walk and—"

"*The property passed to my eldest brother after our parents died there. I ran the pension for a few years after that, but, um...guest numbers never recovered. Just lost money by keeping it open. My brother tried to sell. No one wanted a secluded pension near that valley. Too many...stories. Last I knew, he was never able to find a buyer. That was ten years ago. Thought it was abandoned. How does it look?*"

"It doesn't look abandoned. There's no one around, but the gate is open, the grounds are in decent shape, and if I had to guess, I'd say someone's trimming the vines."

"*What vines?*"

"Around the second and third floors. Looks nicer than some of the buildings in the village."

"Might be squatters. A lot of peculiar folk around there. Those mountains. Either that or my brother sold the place and kept the money for himself. That would explain the Range Rover... Son of a bitch! I'll kill the treacherous snake! He's a communist, you know. A North Korean sympathizer, and a pervert!"

"Uh, okay. Sorry to have bothered you, ma'am. And thanks."

"If you find the owner, call me back. I'll have to get in touch with my sleazy, redback, cocksucker brother—"

The woman hangs up. Eliza and Tae-wook stare at each other, then break down in laughter. Their howling gets Hobbes riled up. He barks and leaps between them, his tail swishing like crazy.

When Eliza passes the leash back to Tae-wook, a curious squealing sound emerges from somewhere on the property. Startled, they look up and, in the confusion, both lose hold of the leash.

Hobbes's ears perk up. He cranks his head over his shoulder, then darts off through the gate.

"Shit!" says Eliza.

"Hobbes!" Tae-wook runs in after him.

Eliza glances around nervously. They haven't seen another soul since leaving the village proper. There are no signs specifically warning against trespassers, so she takes a deep breath and enters the property. Since she doesn't have a chance in hell of catching Hobbes, she slows to a fast walk, merely trying to keep them in sight.

Hobbes races toward the garden, but then cuts back, speeding past Tae-wook, who skids on the gravel and falls over trying to redirect. He sees Eliza and holds up his hand, implying he's got it under control. Hobbes runs around the open space to the left of the house before disappearing behind the building. Tae-wook, having overstretched his hamstring when he fell, limps after him.

Eliza is left alone. She can hear Tae-wook calling the dog, but she can't see either of them. In case he needs help, she strolls toward the back, gazing up at the house as she approaches.

It has a wrap-around porch with evenly spaced trellises. The woodwork looks old, but sturdy and decorative; almost looks hand-carved. The planks are warped, and one set of stairs is seriously crooked. The trellises are devoid of plants, which is strange because vines are prevalent on the upper floors and roof. At first glance, the building's wood siding is painted white. Upon closer inspection, it's more yellowish. Off-white that may be intentional or may be the effects of age. The awnings and windowsills are done in a pale blue that doesn't look dirty at all.

Perhaps the most unconventional thing about the house is the roof. Though steeply angled in the Western fashion, the shingles are the same clay tiles generally found on traditional Korean temples.

Behind the house, Tae-wook screams. "Hobbes, stop!"

The dog runs into view again, happily sprinting along the gravel before turning and heading toward the rear of the lot. Tae-wook hobbles after him, breathing heavily as he pauses and gives Eliza a pathetic look.

"Might need some help, after all…"

Eliza smirks and nods. As she starts toward him, she glances at the house again and abruptly stops.

Something moved.

She stares at the window of the curved corner alcove, positive that she just saw someone. A white curtain covers half the window, the interior beyond is shrouded in darkness, and no one is there now, but she is sure someone just ducked out of view.

They were watching her.

A wriggling worm of fear slinks along her spine.

"Eliza! Come back here!"

Tae-wook and Hobbes are nowhere to be seen. The window remains empty, the curtain unmoved, no sign that anyone is there. She waits another beat, almost expecting someone to open the front door, but no one does.

"Hurry up!" Tae-wook urges from somewhere in the trees. "You gotta see this!"

Several other structures blend into the forest behind the secondary building. A well-trodden dirt path leads past an open-air shelter that could be used for cookouts. Eliza finds Tae-wook and Hobbes beside the next structure, which appears to be a small stable. The doors only come up to belly height. Hobbes is standing with his paws on top, sniffing aggressively and gazing inside. Tae-wook hears Eliza coming and turns to her with a mystified expression.

Before she reaches the stable, she hears grunts and squeals from inside. The smell of shit is overpowering.

She ruffles Hobbes's fur, peers over the doors. Her breath hitches.

"What the hell? What are they?"

"Wild boars, I think. Babies."

"Not wild if they're kept in a pen."

"Yeah... They're not regular hogs, though."

"There's what, twenty of them? Must be two litters. Maybe three. Where did they come from? Where are the sows?"

Both Eliza and Tae-wook glance around. Other than the wind whisking through the leaves and the porcine babble, the woods are quiet. Another structure stands farther along the path. It's hard to tell what it is through the trees, but it doesn't look like a barn or stable.

Hobbes whines and dances around, eager to jump over the half-door and join the juvenile boars. Tae-wook tugs the leash, drags him away. Eliza takes another look, trembling at the sight of the animals. They're just babies, and yet they have coarse, wiry, dark hair, some of them are as big as toddlers, and...

"Tae...? Should baby boars have tusks?"

"I don't think so. Why?"

"Some of them do."

They stand there for a while, away from the stable but still on the path, trying to wrap their heads around what they have found. Hobbes sits, panting, his eyes darting around the surrounding woods as though he hears something they don't.

"Is it legal?" says Eliza.

"Legal gray area, probably. Like everything else in this country. Most people would probably thank them."

"What do they do with them?"

Tae-wook shrugs. "Eat them? Pork is pork, and free pork is best."

"Do the people in the village know?"

"How would I know, Eliza?" snaps Tae-wook. Then, softer, "This is my first time seeing anything like this, too, you know. That shelter, there," he points at the long, open-air structure, "looks like the sort of place you host large parties. Maybe there's, like, an annual Aie Valley cookout, food provided by the valley itself. Or something like that."

Neither of them thinks this is probable. The folks of Aie Valley, for the most part, seem like they prefer keeping to themselves.

A crow calls nearby. Eliza jumps. Tae-wook searches the trees, unable to locate the bird.

"Let's get out of here, Tae."

"Okay," he smiles. "But...I just want to follow this path a little farther. There are—"

"Tae-wook!"

"It'll take two minutes, Lizzie. Might even give us some answers," he jerks a thumb at the stable.

"You were right," she grumbles. "I don't think we're supposed to be here..."

But Tae-wook and Hobbes are already walking ahead, following the path past the stable, deeper into the wooded property. Eliza follows reluctantly.

The trail winds its way through the trees. Densely forested land rises sharply on either side, forming a small valley, an offshoot of the much larger Aie Valley. A rickety wooden bridge with no rails carries them over a stream, and soon they come upon the next structure. A Korean-style grotto.

While Eliza walks around the sides, examining the woodwork and shoddy paint job—too much pale blue, just like the house—Tae-wook and Hobbes step inside. It's raised high off the ground, and the masonry forming the foundation looks ancient. The wood creaks beneath their weight.

"Did you ever see anything like this?" Tae-wook says. He's pointing upward at the center of the grotto's roof.

Eliza comes closer to the edge, her head just about level with the floorboards, which Hobbes is sniffing with unusual intensity. In the center of the roof, there's a hole roughly a meter across. The shape is irregular but appears to have been cut out on purpose.

"No, never," answers Eliza. "What would be the point of that?"

"Natural shower?" suggests Tae-wook with a stuttering, uncertain laughter.

Eliza lowers her gaze to look more closely at the floorboards, where she sees the faint traces of tracks.

"Tae...look down."

Squinting, he squats for a closer look.

"Are those what I think they are?" Eliza asks, backing away.

"Yeah, I think so. Two toes. Definitely not from the babies, though. These are full-sized."

"So, what, the sows are free range and just come here to give birth?"

"I guess so."

"I'm being sarcastic, Tae. It's fucking weird. Can we go now?"

Tae-wook glances down the trail and sighs. He sees no more structures, but there is something. A boulder that's been intentionally placed. Possibly a headstone. He peers through the branches, but all he can tell for sure is that it's in an open glade, full of sunlight. The look on his wife's face, however, warns him against investigating. He can always come back later on his own.

"Yeah, come on—"

Rustling sounds in the trees behind Eliza. They all hear it and go rigid. Eliza steps away, coming closer to the grotto. Tae-wook stands still, but he's craning his neck to see whatever is moving in the bushes. Hobbes's ears are perked up, his posture straight as a rod, a rumbling growl issuing from his throat. They wait, expecting to hear more.

Hobbes barks.

"Quiet, Hobbes!" hisses Eliza.

"No, let him," says Tae-wook. "Making noise will scare it away."

"They might consider this their territory." Eliza indicates the prints on the grotto floor.

"Right," Tae-wook agrees. "Come on, boy."

As soon as he starts down the stairs, Hobbes shoots forward. Tae-wook miraculously keeps his balance, staggering down the steps as Hobbes dashes across the path. With a yank on the leash, Tae-wook stops the dog from dragging him into the trees.

"Hobbes! Hobbes! Stop it!" Tae-wook has both hands on the leash now. He's pulling as hard as he can, his face red, veins bulging in his neck as Hobbes lunges forward. The dog is head-deep in a barberry bush, sniffing like crazy. Tae-wook looks pleadingly at Eliza. "A little help here?"

Eliza goes to him but stops before she gets there, her mouth broken in a silent scream. A long, dark-colored appendage—Arm? Tail? Vine? Tentacle?—darts between the branches, latches onto Hobbes, and pulls with astounding force. The leash is torn from Tae-wook's grasp. Hobbes whimpers for a moment, then goes quiet as the leash disappears into the bush like an alarmed snake.

Swift footsteps retreat into the forest, crunching atop fallen branches and dead leaves.

Just like that, their dog is gone.

"Tae-wook! What the fuck was that?"

"I didn't see," Tae-wook says, looking stunned. "Did he run in there?"

"Something took him!"

"Something?"

"Hobbes!" Eliza, her eyes wild, races into the woods.

"Damnit, Liz! Wait!"

She gets tangled in the branches, and Tae-wook has to pull her out. The footsteps fade, blending into the sound of leaves in a sudden gust of wind. As Tae-wook drags Eliza away, she struggles to free herself. He keeps shushing her, trying to quiet her down so he can hear which direction the footsteps are moving. When her heel lands sharply on his shin, he finally lets go.

"What the hell, Tae? Why are you just standing there?"

"Will you calm down?" He's wincing, bent over, rubbing his ankle.

"Fuck you! Something just took the dog! We have to—"

"Nothing took him. I just lost my grip. He jumped so suddenly."

"No, I saw—"

A chorus of squeals erupts from the stable. The boarlets have become agitated. Tae-wook, thinking it's probably Hobbes causing the disturbance, runs back along the path. As he crosses the wooden bridge, he glances back, shooting Eliza an urgent glare.

But Eliza stays put. She knows what she saw.

Actually, no—she doesn't have a clue what she saw. But she knows she saw *something*.

She remains by the grotto, peering into the trees. Tae-wook is calling the dog's name. The baby boars abruptly settle down. Deep in the forest, something moves among the trees. It might be a swaying branch and it might be Hobbes. Eliza has a bad feeling about this, but she can't just leave her dog to whatever or whoever is out there. Without Tae-wook by her side, she feels particularly vulnerable. What's a small woman like her going to do if an angry, territorial boar bares its tusks and charges?

A hand lands on Eliza's shoulder. She screams.

"It's me!" says Tae-wook, tearing his arm away.

Eliza glares at him, then back into the forest.

It sinks in suddenly—Hobbes is gone. Tears well in her eyes. She falls sobbing into Tae-wook's arms.

"What are we going to do?"

"I don't know," he sighs. "He'll come out eventually. Maybe he can find his way home? Otherwise, someone will find him. He has his tags."

"We have to call someone."

"Who can we—" Tae-wook stops himself, knowing this will only upset her more. "Alright, yeah." He takes out his phone, stares at it, holds it up. "There's no signal. We have to go back to the pension."

The trail has become supremely tranquil. The burbling of the stream, the breeze through the leaves, birds fluttering and chirping in the trees. Eliza gets her breathing under control and manages to staunch her tears. Tae-wook leads her, his arm around her waist. The baby boars sense their approach and produce a gentle murmur. There's an uncanny stillness in the air, and daylight is rapidly fading.

When they get to the open-air shelter, they both notice certain details and pause. The concrete slab looks recent. Neither the steel posts nor the wooden awning shows any signs of age. Looking down at the dirt path, they see the same cloven-hoofed footprints they saw at the grotto.

Passing by the secondary building, they return to the gravel lot. Flies buzz around a compost heap near the edge of the forest.

Eliza disengages from Tae-wook's arm. "Hobbes! Hobbes! Come here, boy! Hobbes!"

She skirts along the edge of the woods while Tae-wook wanders around the parking lot holding up his phone. It's not until he's near the main house that he gets a signal. He sits down on the porch steps and dials the police.

After rooting around near the trees awhile, Eliza returns to the house. Tae-wook is gone.

"Tae? Tae!" Her voice cracks with alarm.

The wood creaks with slow footsteps. Eliza backs away, her eyes darting from one window to the next, lingering long on the door. The sensation that she's being watched grows stronger with each passing second. Whomever she saw in the window before is still there, just out of sight.

A moment later, Tae-wook comes strolling around the corner of the porch, the wood groaning under his weight.

"This place is so weird," he says. "Maybe it is abandoned. There's nothing here. No evidence of any people. I peeked in the windows. Totally dark. No furniture."

"There's someone in there. I saw them."

"What? When?"

"When you were chasing Hobbes."

"Are you sure?"

Eliza hesitates. "Yes, I'm sure."

Tae-wook stares at her a moment, then turns away. He goes right up to the door, knocks loudly. "Hello? Anyone home?" He leans over to peer through a window, raps on the pane, and listens. Then he tries the doorknob. "Locked," he says, shaking his head as he descends the stairs. "I don't know, Liz. I don't think there's anyone here."

"I know what I saw."

"Maybe it was one of the Aie Valley ghosts everyone keeps talking about."

"Oh, what? And it was a ghost that snatched Hobbes?"

Tae-wook doesn't reply; he just smirks and looks away.

"You don't believe me?" she sneers.

"I didn't say that. But you know how he is. When he wants to go after something, there's no stopping him. And...I don't know what to tell you. I didn't see anything."

"Asshole," mutters Eliza. "What did the cops say?"

"They're on their way." Tae-wook sits on the steps as Eliza storms back to the woods, screaming Hobbes's name.

Fifteen minutes later, a squad car rolls up to the gate. It parks outside. The two officers take their time getting out. When they do, they stop at the edge of the property. Tae-wook calls Eliza. She jogs over to him by the porch, and they stand there staring at the cops, who only stare back at them from the entrance.

"You the ones who called?" shouts the taller of the two officers.

Tae-wook looks at Eliza, shrugs, and takes her hand as they walk toward the gate.

"I called, yes," says Tae-wook.

The second officer is short, no taller than Eliza, and much older. He ignores them as they approach, examining the fence and gate instead.

The first officer, younger, steps forward to meet them. He's gazing at his feet, careful not to step onto the property. "What's the problem?"

"It's our dog," says Tae-wook.

The officer raises his eyebrows, waiting.

"Something took him," adds Eliza. Tae-wook sighs, but she ignores him. "Back there. In the woods behind the pension."

The tall officer gazes at Eliza in wonder, clearly not expecting the white woman to speak Korean.

Tae-wook starts to explain. "We don't *know* that something took him, but we were—"

"What are you doing here?" The short officer cuts him off, his voice stern, gruff, and phlegmy. He's still not looking at them, but pulling on the gate, apparently checking to see if it's stuck.

"Just, uh...walking the dog," stutters Tae-wook.

"You live in the village?" asks the tall officer, his tone more measured.

"Yes," says Tae-wook. "Moved in two weeks ago."

The older cop scoffs and finally looks at them, leveling a spiteful glare at Eliza. "Shouldn't be here."

"Excuse me?" snaps Eliza. "I have every right to live where I want."

The tall cop holds up his hands, a genial smile on his lips that looks anything but sincere. "What my partner means is that this is private property. Can I ask...how did you get inside?"

"The gate was open," says Tae-wook, acid in his voice now, too. "And there's no sign but that one. How were we to know it's private property? Besides, there's no one here."

The officers exchange a look.

"Are you going to help us find our dog or what?" spits Eliza.

The tall officer sighs and turns to her. "You say someone stole your dog?"

"Possibly," Tae-wook answers hastily. "My wife isn't sure what she saw. He might have just run off into the forest."

Both officers stare at Tae-wook, squinting slightly. The younger one shows his upturned palms as if to say, *What do you expect us to do about it?*

"I know what I fucking saw," Eliza seethes.

"And what was that?" says the older cop.

"It was a..." She glances at Tae-wook, then over her shoulder at the house. "An arm, I think. A long, dark arm. Out of a bush. It grabbed Hobbes, hauled him into the trees, and then ran off. Up the mountain."

"A human arm?" asks the tall officer.

Eliza shrugs. "I guess. What else could it be?"

"Color and breed?"

"Black Jindo," responds Tae-wook.

"Black arm, black dog?" The officer peers at him suspiciously. "How convenient."

"Also, we found a stable full of wild hogs out back. Babies. Someone must be trapping them or—"

"And there's someone in the house," adds Eliza. "I saw them."

The short cop clears his throat and steps forward. Like his partner, he's careful to avoid stepping on the gravel. "That doesn't surprise me. As we've already informed you, this is private property. The owners do not appreciate being disturbed. Neither do we, for that matter. Missing pets are no concern of the police. If your dog ran away, that's your problem. These mountains are well-known for being hazardous. Search for the mutt if you like, but we do not recommend it. If you get lost, we won't come looking for you. You'll be on your own unless the owners of the Aie Valley Pension happen upon you. Then, well…let's just say you may wish you hadn't been found."

The officer stares at them with leaden eyes, his glare lingering longer on Eliza. Abruptly, he heads back to the squad car. The tall officer smiles, gesturing that they should come along.

"Wait!" Eliza shouts. "Are you saying the owners will do something to our dog? And you're just going to let it happen?"

"Listen, Miss America," barks the short cop. "The owners of this property have lived in this valley for generations. I know for a fact that they do not want your kind around here, especially not trespassing on their land. They do things their own way, always have, but they do not step on our toes, so we don't step on theirs. You don't belong here, lady, and it's not our fault that you have no control over your animal. You want our help? Then take our advice and get the hell out of here."

"Fucking pig," Eliza mutters, slipping into English and not caring whether the officer understands or not.

As soon as she mutters the words, a huge, vile grin spreads across the cop's face. He lets out a churlish, scornful laughter and opens the passenger door. "Officer Shin, get in the car."

The door slams.

The tall officer gazes at them apologetically. "I'm sorry, but my partner is right. You really shouldn't be here. And if your dog is lost in these mountains, I'm afraid the chances of recovering it are slim. If you'd like, we can give you a lift back to the village."

"Jesus Christ!" Eliza screams and stomps away, back into the property.

Tae-wook steps closer to Officer Shin, speaking low. "They're an old family? Old customs?"

The officer says nothing.

"Are you saying..." Tremors render Tae-wook's voice unsteady. He glances back, making sure Eliza is out of earshot. "Are you saying they'll eat him? Dog meat stew?"

Officer Shin shakes his head. "What we're saying is that you do not want to know. You need to leave." He stares over Tae-wook's shoulder at Eliza, who is jogging toward the woods. Then, he gazes sharply at Tae-wook, meeting his eyes. "Leave now. Do not look for your dog."

"I understand," Tae-wook sighs. "I'll get her out of here. Thank you, officer. And sorry for—"

The officer holds up his hand to stop Tae-wook. He gives a weak smile before hurrying to the squad car. As the car reverses down the lane, Tae-wook sees the older officer shaking his head in disapproval. Then, Tae-wook runs to catch up to his wife.

He follows her voice, past the open-air shelter, past the stable of squealing boarlets, all the way to the grotto where Hobbes went missing. Eliza has gone off the path. He hears her calling to the dog but can't see her, can't even place her. With no idea which direction she's gone or exactly how deep into the woods she is, he figures it's better not to risk both of them getting lost.

But how long can he realistically wait? The sun is already going down. Daylight fades quickly in the forest. Once it gets dark, their chances of finding Hobbes will be almost nil. Tae-wook is thirsty, hungry, wishing they were at home, all three of them. They should be lounging around, preparing dinner, easing into their beautiful new home, this second chapter of their married life.

Tae-wook sits on the steps of the grotto and buries his head in his hands. Eliza's voice has grown more distant, and it sounds like she's losing hope. She loves the dog, picked him out herself. They've had Hobbes since before the wedding. He is a fixture in their life. There will be no replacing him. Without Hobbes, he knows, Eliza will spiral into a depression. Their life will never be the same. Their marriage is strong, but...can it withstand a blow like that?

Tae-wook isn't sure it can.

He keeps returning to what those police officers said—no, what they *didn't say*. What they had *implied*. The people who own this land have "lived in this valley for generations." So, they what? Don't like foreigners? Don't like people moving here from the city? Don't suffer uninvited guests? And they "do things their own way." What the hell is that supposed to mean? They steal people's pets and eat them along with the feral pigs they trap in the mountains?

Maybe Tae-wook and Eliza shouldn't have left the city. When they first came to view the condo, they both got eerie vibes from Aie Valley. It seemed too calm, too quiet, like it was severed from the regular flow of time. Everyone they encountered that day stared at them as though they were from another planet. They both put this down to the expected reactions of rural folk when encountering a blonde-haired white girl, even though Aie Valley can barely be considered rural. It's just outside Seoul. And, as they later learned, several other foreigners reside in the village. After seeing and falling in love with the condo, they forgot all about those initial reservations. It seemed like the perfect, quaint place to slow down their lives and relax a little, with the added advantage of giving Hobbes more range to run, frolic, piss, and shit.

These first two weeks have been bliss. Without Hobbes, though, this perfect life might just transform into a living nightmare.

A branch snaps behind the grotto. Tae-wook stands up and peers through the railing.

"Anybody there?" Something moves among the trees, but there are no footsteps. A shadow. Perhaps a ghost. "Hobbes?"

Nothing.

Tae-wook shakes his head, looks nervously at the darkening sky through the branches above, then heads off down the path. He comes to another stream. The bridge here is made of old, cut stones that look like they're from the Joseon Era. It's solid but narrow with no railings. He assumes it's the same stream, winding back and forth over the property, but this section is deeper. To the right of the bridge, it almost looks like the banks have been intentionally widened to form a pond.

"Eliza!"

A clawing anxiety digs its nails into Tae-wook's stomach when he realizes he can no longer hear his wife's voice. Moving faster, he ignores the shadows in the trees, telling himself it's just the low light, there's no way he's being followed. The next structure is just ahead, a stone marker with two wooden totems straddling it. The trail mounts a small hill before steeply descending on the other side. A few more paces onward, Tae-wook stumbles into a clearing.

The trees here have been cut down to stumps, manicured like natural stools, or maybe pedestals. At the center is a monument unlike anything Tae-wook has ever seen. A three-meter-tall stone tablet stands elevated on a wide stone platform. The Chinese characters carved into the face are largely incomprehensible to Tae-wook, nothing like what he had to study in school. The few he recognizes don't seem to belong together. *Procreation* is one. *Conquer*, another. *Conquer nature? Conquer nations?* Several characters repeatedly appear together, and they seem to mean something along the lines of *Feed the young, march on the future.*

The totems to either side of the tablet are unlike the *jangseungs* scattered around the village. These are not carved with images but covered with more Chinese characters in auburn paint. Tae-wook can make no sense of these except to infer that they offer some sort of warning. On top of each totem sits a crow. They look alive, but neither is moving. After a few moments, he realizes they're just expertly preserved.

Most perplexing of all is the stone basin at his feet. He stands at the edge of an enormous, flat boulder, at least five times as big as the tablet. In the middle is a shallow depression that might be natural, except it's too uniform, a perfect oval. Definitely not natural are the drainage channels crudely carved into it, leading out of the depression into a circular gutter with twelve off-shooting reservoirs.

"What the—"

"*Tae-wook!*"

Eliza's scream is far away but so hysterical and high-pitched that it cuts through the forest. Tae-wook jumps, his head jerking toward the sound. He looks up, seeing that the sky has transitioned to evening purples and pinks. It will be dark within twenty minutes. Without thinking, he plunges into the woods.

"*Eliza!*"

After ten minutes, his voice is so hoarse that he can't shout anymore. A dim glow still illuminates above the trees, but the forest is buried in murky darkness. Gradually, her voice gets louder. He can hear her stomping through the fallen leaves, though every once in a while he's thrown off by footsteps from another direction.

He stops, listening and clearing his throat so he can attempt to call out again. Something runs past to his right. All he sees is a dark blur, low to the ground.

"Hobbes?" He whispers to save his voice. "Shit..."

If it's the dog, he's so close. But if it's not...then what the hell is it?

"Tae-wook?"

Her voice is not so frantic this time, and it lilts up into a question. He steps forward, scanning the darkness.

"Eliza! Over here—" A coughing fit cuts him off, but he waves his arms and sprints toward her. Every other step, his feet find a fallen log or branch. Somehow, he manages to keep his balance.

They meet, and Tae-wook wraps his arms around her. Her cheeks glisten with tears, she's out of breath, and she pushes out of his embrace.

"We need to get out of here right now," she says, urging him back the way he came. "Is this right? This way?"

He nods and takes her hand. "What, Liz? What is it?"

"Something's fucking chasing me!"

As she says it, they hear footsteps and a throaty rumbling vocalization nearby. Not quite a growl and not quite a bark, but something in between.

"Shit. It's the mother," says Tae-wook.

"What?"

"A boar. You go first. This way…I think…"

"You don't know?"

"It's dark! Just run!"

In the low light and dense underbrush, a true run is impossible. They are constantly tripping, snagging on branches, and plowing into tree trunks. On one of his falls, Tae-wook picks up a hefty, club-like branch. He brandishes it like a tennis racket, swinging uselessly whenever he spies a shadow or hears movement other than their own.

The creature following them moves in spurts. It allows them to get ahead before crashing madly through the forest, almost as though it wants to be heard. And it's not just pursuing from behind. It moves with such unhindered speed that it keeps encroaching on either side. Forest shrubs tremble to their left and right, small trees bend sideways, branches are flung this way and that. The panoramic crunch of dead leaves whirls ceaselessly around them.

If it wants to attack, it has every opportunity.

They are not being chased. They are being herded.

Eliza slips on the muddy bank of a stream. Tae-wook helps her up and pulls her along, following the flow of the water. The ground is relatively flat now, which means they're off the mountain slope. The stream leads them back to the trail, and Tae-wook recognizes the stone bridge. He directs Eliza to the right, away from the sinister monument.

Back on the trail, they can move much faster. They're sore and banged up from numerous falls, but they've sustained no serious injuries. They run holding hands, neither realizing how insanely tight they're squeezing. Their pursuer seems to have backed off. They can hear nothing crashing through the woods, no footsteps following them on the path. Tae-wook glances back and thinks he sees a figure crouched on the stone bridge, but he convinces himself it's only a shadow.

Darkness consumes the path. Gaps in the branches above reveal a metallic sky.

Just ahead, on their left, is the grotto. As they pass by, Eliza gasps and her legs give out. She spills to her knees. Tae-wook roughly picks her up, glancing at the grotto as he does so.

His blood freezes. Guttural terror sweeps his mind blank.

Shrouded in the darkness of the grotto stands a tall, hairy figure. A faint ray of moonlight shines through the hole in the roof, revealing a face that cannot be real. The figure remains perfectly still, but it's watching them.

Tae-wook drags Eliza onward.

"Did you..." wheezes Eliza. "Did you see that?"

"Yeah."

"What the fuck was it?"

"A person..."

"That was not a person, Tae. Didn't you see its face?"

"It's a mask. Has to be. Just come on."

"What about Hobbes?"

Tae-wook shakes his head. "Lizzie... We have to go."

As Eliza crosses the narrow wooden bridge, the planks emit a loud, grinding crack. The bridge buckles but doesn't break. Eliza wobbles, regains her balance, and hops across. Tae-wook takes a deep breath and backs up a step. Light on his feet, he runs forward, the wood crumbling away underneath as he throws himself into Eliza's arms. After a quick embrace, they gaze down at the fallen bridge, feeling a sort of moral victory, like whatever has been chasing them and whatever was watching from the grotto will not be able to follow in pursuit.

This is total bullshit, of course, and they both know it. The stream is neither deep nor wide. Anyone or anything could simply wade across. When they take off running down the final stretch of the path, they move with just as much haste as before. Even faster, perhaps, since escape now seems within reach.

A strangely inflected grunting noise makes them jump as they race past the stable. A crouched figure slowly rises amid the pitch-dark inside, standing even taller than the figure in the grotto. A shadow among shadows, though its piercing eyes glimmer as it watches them. The boarlets blare manically as Tae-wook and Eliza sprint away.

At the open-air shelter, it's Tae-wook who does a double-take and then pauses. Every other time they passed by, the shelter's concrete floor had been empty. Now, candles flicker in the center, and the concrete is covered in what looks like hay.

Eliza jerks Tae-wook onward. They emerge from the woods onto the gravel parking lot, their footsteps grating alarmingly on the rocks. In an unconscious attempt to make less noise, they slow down, careful not to drag their feet. They're out in the open now. To their right is the compost heap and a single tall lamppost that casts a dour yellow light over the barren lot, and beyond that, the yawning darkness of the forest. On the left are the main pension and the secondary building. All the windows are dark, but a single bulb burns dimly on the pension's porch. Although they see no signs of life, it feels as if the darkness itself is watching them, judging them.

Tae-wook looks back, relieved that none of the dark figures from the trail are following. Eliza starts crying, an unnerving combination of thankfulness to have made it out and grief over their lost companion.

They both stare warily at the house as they hurry past. Eliza yelps and stops, tugging on Tae-wook's wrist.

"There." She points at the window beside the door. "I told you. Someone's in there. I saw them again."

"It doesn't matter, Liz. We have to go."

"But what if they have Hobbes?" Her weeping intensifies. Tae-wook is afraid she might have a meltdown right here and now. What is he supposed to do, carry her out slung over his shoulder?

"I'm sorry, but we..."

A slow, creaking sound breaks his concentration.

The front door opens. A dark figure, just like those in the grotto and stable, stands on the threshold.

Tae-wook drags Eliza away, but at the same time, another noise is coming from behind, and she's trying to pull him back toward the woods. It sounds like their unseen pursuer, trampling over fallen branches and dead leaves, plowing over shrubs, breathing its wet, savage breaths as it bursts out of the trees beside the compost heap, into the light of the lamppost.

"Hobbes...?" says Eliza, starting towards it.

Tae-wook grabs her wrist. "No, Liz. It's too big. It's a—"

He's about to say it's a boar, because it clearly is, with its high, arched back, its coarse, bristly fur, its low, swaying head and two massive tusks. But his words escape him, his mouth agape, breathless as the animal rises onto its hind legs without breaking stride. Standing erect, it walks with a vaguely human gait. Broad-shouldered, its arms sway at its sides, its steps are long but jerky, its considerable phallus and testes bouncing from side to side.

The creature does not run but comes directly at them, swiftly covering the distance.

Tae-wook and Eliza let go of each other's hands so they can run without hindrance. Past the house, across the gravel lot, toward the iron fence at the front of the property, where the narrow road leads back to the village. The safety of home.

The gate.

Is fucking.

Closed.

"No, no, no!" Tae-wook yells, summoning a burst of excess speed that sends him ahead of Eliza and crashing into the iron posts. His face slams into a bar, opening a deep gash on his chin. His upper teeth slice into his lip, blood filling his mouth and dripping onto his chest. Pointlessly, he grabs and shakes the heavy bars.

"What are we going to do?" Eliza wails, frantic as she joins him rattling the gate.

Tae-wook is pulling, pushing, pounding, searching for the point at which the gate should swing open. When he finds it, the air is sucked out of him. The chain securing the gate is as fat as a python, the padlock as big as his fist. His shoulders slump. He looks up, trying to determine whether they can climb over.

"Tae..."

Eliza's voice sounds distant. Tae-wook is still shaking the gate, but his energy sags and his mind sputters like a dying engine, offering no solutions. Still, he refuses to simply give up.

"Tae..."

The gap underneath the bars is too narrow for them to fit through. Looking up again, he thinks maybe he can hoist Eliza over. Then, if he can only make it into the pension, maybe he can find a place to hide, possibly a weapon to defend himself. And he still has his phone to call for help and—

"Tae-wook, look!"

The cutting pitch of Eliza's voice fills Tae-wook with dread. He turns, squinting to minimize the shock of something he knows he doesn't want to see. Eliza runs to his side, latching on with obscene strength. Tremors flow through her body. Together, they back away and are stopped by the gate.

The upright boar that emerged from the woods has been joined by others. Dozens of boar-people are advancing on them. They emerge from the house's front door, some descending the steps and others gathering on the porch. Groups of them stream out from behind the building, half walking upright, half trotting on all fours. Still more are slinking out of the woods on both sides. There must be fifty of them, all staring at Tae-wook and Eliza as they close in.

"What do you want with us?!"

Eliza's piercing voice aggravates them, their silence swelling into a cacophony of grunts and squeals.

Tae-wook wraps his arm around his wife. They both cower against the cold iron. Now that the creatures are close, surrounding them in a tight semicircle, he can no longer convince himself that they're just people donning grotesque masks. They all have tails, fur covers their bodies, and their nauseating, feral stink is enough to make him retch.

Their squeals rise to a deafening crescendo, then taper off as a final, immense figure steps from the pension. The others move aside as it approaches, carving a path directly toward the shuddering couple. This one is at least a head taller than the others. Its legs are like tree trunks, its tusks as long as carving knives.

As it studies Tae-wook and Eliza, it commands silence by producing a series of throaty grunts with breaks and pauses that sound disturbingly like human speech.

"We're...we're sorry for...for coming onto your land," stutters Tae-wook. Spurred on by the alpha's silent attention, he squeezes Eliza closer and continues. "We didn't know, and we...we meant no harm. Please, let us go. We won't...we won't...we won't tell anybody about you. And we won't...we won't come back here. Ever. You have our word..."

The boar-people in the rear become restless. Growls, barks, and long, wavering squeals rise and fall. The alpha looks from side to side, emitting a harsh cough-like groan that instantly silences the others. It steps closer, towering over Tae-wook and Eliza, then starts again with another long series of squeals and barks. This time, they both recognize certain instances of inflection, emphasis, and even pitch changes.

"Is it talking?" whispers Eliza. "Can it understand us?"

"I don't know," says Tae-wook. "I think so."

Before Tae-wook can stop her, Eliza jerks out of his grasp and throws herself to her knees, bowing low before the giant boar.

"Please! *Plee-eee-ease!*" she wails.

"Eliza..." whispers Tae-wook anxiously.

"Please give us back our dog! Let us take him! *Plee-ease!*"

To Tae-wook's surprise, Eliza's groveling appears to have drawn a reaction from the great boar. Thinking it might be her submissive posture, Tae-wook kneels beside her, bowing before the creature. While he's down there, he sees that their feet are nothing like human feet. They are two-toed trotters. Hog's feet.

The giant boar leans over them, sniffing the backs of their necks. The warm, moist air from its snout smells of rotten meat and feels like death's foreboding touch.

Then, the creature growls directly above their ears. It's so loud and intimidating that they both scuttle backward until they're pressed into the gate again. The boar makes a human-like gesture with its two-toed hands, demanding that they rise to their feet. When they do, another boar steps forward with something dangling from its extended foreleg.

Hobbes's leash.

Eliza lets out a miserable moan. The boar-people respond en masse with a dreadful caterwauling of squeals. The alpha boar takes the leash and holds it aloft, barking menacingly. The others wind down to silence once more.

Tae-wook pulls Eliza to his side, whispering nonsense into her ear. He's crying now, too, and can't seem to put words together.

The alpha boar then makes a different, unexpected vocalization. A high-pitched whine followed by an almost canine bark.

Light, quick footsteps approach through the gravel. A black shape weaves between the forest of legs.

"Hobbes!" shouts Eliza.

Their dog emerges from the herd. He hears his name, sees his owners, and tilts his head.

"Come, boy," whimpers Tae-wook. "Here, Hobbes."

The dog approaches tentatively until the alpha boar repeats its harsh bark. Instantly, Hobbes turns away to face the creature. He sits at attention, staring into the monster's beady and eerily human eyes. The boar points at the gate, grunting, barking, and snarling, and Hobbes obeys at once. He ignores Eliza and Tae-wook, instead prowling along the perimeter of the fence, his gaze directed at the road beyond.

Crestfallen, Eliza and Tae-wook gape at their pet, not believing, not willing to accept what is happening. Neither of them hears the next series of grunts or the approaching footsteps.

Filthy, mud-encrusted trotters grab them, drag them away from the gate, and immobilize them while another boar steps forward with the leash. One end is tied around Tae-wook's neck and the other around Eliza's. They choke and gasp for breath. The same boar holds the leash in the center and tugs sharply until they follow.

The herd of boar-people parts, observing as Tae-wook and Eliza are mercilessly dragged across the gravel lot, past the house, and back onto the trail leading into the woods.

The boar drops onto all fours, trotting between them with the leash clamped in its mouth. It moves at a brisk pace, forcing them to jog alongside it. At one point, Eliza drops to her knees in an attempt to resist. She lies prostrate, but the boar's momentum is not affected in the slightest. She is simply dragged along the ground, the leash tightening around her neck until she can no longer breathe and is compelled to rise to her feet again. Then, Tae-wook trips over a rock, and the same thing happens. Choking and losing air, he flails to regain his feet.

The herd has fallen in behind them, all the boar-people following this vulgar procession into the darkness. Far ahead, deep in the woods, Tae-wook spots the flickering light of a blaze.

The boarlets release a demented squall as Tae-wook and Eliza are led past the stable. Three huge, unmoving boar-people stand on the grotto platform, observing the passing herd.

At the stone bridge, they stop and wait for the others to crowd in around them. A few of the boars step forward to grab Tae-wook and Eliza by the arms and shove them into the widened section of the stream. Rough, hairy, two-toed hands submerge them. Sharp teeth rip and tear at their clothing. The sensation of tusks pressing against their flesh renders them both motionless with fear, all fight drained away. But the teeth do not penetrate their skin. Instead, they are stripped nude, their garments shredded off in a matter of seconds.

Eliza weeps as wet trotters and coarse-grained tongues scrape at her flesh. Tae-wook is past crying or screaming; he's in shock, unable to take his eyes off the morbid scene and yet unable to react. He doesn't want to know what is in store for them; he wishes these monstrous aberrations of nature would cut this humiliation short and put them out of their misery. He has an idea of where they are being taken, but only a terrified guess as to the purpose.

When the couple has been sufficiently scrubbed, the procession continues over the bridge and along the remaining trail until they arrive at the place Tae-wook has been dreading ever since he stumbled upon it.

The path opens upon the clearing where the stone tablet looms over the proceedings. A bonfire burns on the platform at the tablet's base, illuminating the entire glade. The firelight grants lifelike motion to the stuffed crows atop the warning totems. Below lies the immense stone basin, empty, cold, and hard. Lit torches are rammed into the earth around the perimeter, casting ghoulish shadows that dance around the encircling tree trunks.

The boar-people, eerily silent now, shuffle into the clearing. They crowd around the stone basin, squeezing into a tight, predetermined formation. The alpha boar mounts the platform, taking its position of prominence beneath the tablet. The flames light its face from below, accentuating its grotesque features. Enormous tusks jut from its lower lip, curving threateningly beside its long snout. Discolored saliva drips from its maw. When all the others have taken their places, the alpha raises its arms skyward with a devilish squeal.

A violent tug at the leash pulls Tae-wook and Eliza forward. Naked, dripping, and sniveling, they are crudely thrown into the concave, elliptical basin. Though the stone is surprisingly smooth, it still scrapes their flesh when they land. Blood runs from their knees and hands, sending the boar-people into a frenzy only quelled by a wicked-sounding grunt from the alpha. The boar with the leash jerks it, roughly pulling them onto their sides. Facing one another, all they see is each other's fear. Eliza is no longer sobbing, but steady streams of tears roll down her cheeks. Though Tae-wook cannot hear her voice, he sees her lips moving and understands what she is trying to say.

"Tae-wook... Tae-wook... I love you..."

A final thrust of urgent rebellion surges within him, a violent necessity to protect his wife. Growling and foaming at the mouth, he scratches and pulls at the leash until the knot comes undone. He slips it off his neck, simultaneously sitting up and shifting to a squat, prepared to hurl himself at any perceived threat.

Seeing her husband rise, seeing the ferocious resolve in his expression, Eliza discovers a vein of courage within herself. She, too, rises to her haunches. They share a determined look, firm in their intention to survive.

Two huge, fur-covered bodies launch from either side of the circle, one landing a blow to Tae-wook's temple and the other hitting Eliza in the back of the head. They both crumple onto the stone as a second pair of boar-people bound out, grunting behind them. Both Tae-wook and Eliza see them coming. They kick and thrash their feet, but it's no use. With astounding efficiency and terrifying precision, the boars unleash their tusks on Tae-wook's and Eliza's calves, slicing clear through their Achilles tendons.

They cry out in pain. Any further attempt at standing up fails, each of them repeatedly trying and falling to their knees. Finally, they give up. Blood pools in the depression between them. They reach out to take each other's hands, both of them weeping uncontrollably.

The sight and scent of blood bring on another delirious song of squeals from the herd. Unhinged bloodlust flows around the circle in waves, yet none step into the basin. The boar-people, standing erect with their monstrous bodies, form an impenetrable wall. Shadows play off all those hideous faces, a surreal congregation of slavering beasts. Firelight reflects off their beady, black eyes, and their curled lips are slathered in dripping saliva.

Staring at the unreal sight, suffering under the anguish of waiting for the inevitable, Tae-wook senses fractures forming in his mind. Madness is coming. If this goes on much longer, madness will claim him before death gets the chance. Judging by the wretched, tortured expression carved onto Eliza's face, he thinks her mind may be gone already. He tilts his head to look at his mangled ankles and notices a gap in the circle of boar-people right where they came into the clearing.

The path is still open.

Something else is coming.

The alpha boar emits a string of churlish grunts. Tae-wook looks up. The boar's snout is raised high, pointing at the black, starlit sky, and it lets out an unholy screech that drowns out the others until they join in. Soon, the entire herd is banded together in a maddening howl. On cue, they transition to a chorus of disjointed, boorish barking.

Eliza screams insanely.

Still barking, the boar-people turn their heads to stare at the path. What sounds like a stampede is swiftly approaching.

Tae-wook looks up to find the alpha glaring down at him and Eliza, its lips twisted in a fiendish grin. On the tablet behind the boar's head, lit by the light of the fire, Tae-wook sees a grouping of Chinese characters he recognized earlier.

Feed the young.

"Oh my God..." he mutters, gazing past his feet, where small, shadowy figures emerge over the rise in the path.

Tae-wook joins his wife, screaming and squirming.

The boarlets emerge from the darkness, racing toward them with starved, feverish eyes, some on four legs, some on two, their teeth gnashing and clacking, saliva flying from their open mouths.

In seconds, two dozen tiny monsters are crowded into the stone trough with Tae-wook and Eliza. Grunting, squealing bodies battle for position to dig into their soft parts. Hundreds of teeth slash and rip apart their flesh. Huffing snouts probe their insides. Tusks tear the muscles and tendons from their bones. Blood sprays and flows freely, rapidly filling the basin with a crimson pool. The blood drains along the channels into the twelve offshoots, pouring into the reservoirs. Through the delirious haze of impending death, Tae-wook sees the alpha boar fill a chalice from the basin and raise it like an offering. The adult boar-people take turns dipping their heads to the reservoirs to lap up the blood while their young consume the flesh.

The last thing Tae-wook and Eliza hear is Hobbes howling in the distance.

Acknowledgments

Sometimes story ideas arrive unexpectedly and, from a working standpoint, at awkward times. The stories in this collection are a good example of this phenomenon. With the exception of "Bearded Vulture," they emerged in a flurry of inspiration while I was editing down my forthcoming novel, *The Coyotes' Cross Prowler.* While the composition absolutely delayed my progress on that novel, I wouldn't have it any other way. The creative overlap of working on the two projects simultaneously allowed me to view them each through different lenses, helping me to tighten the bolts and draw out the horror.

First and foremost, I have to thank and credit my amazing wife, Gyubin Song. Not only do I receive her unending support, encouragement, and insight, but this collection in particular would not exist without her. The two stories set in South Korea—"Sea of Ruin" and "The Hogs of Aie Valley"—began to germinate while we were off exploring interesting new places together. Aie Valley is loosely based on the environs of our previous home, and Mangchi Mongdol Beach is a real beach on the southeastern coast of Geoje Island. We often bounce hypotheticals back and forth. Usually, they are outrageous and silly, more in the tone of Monty Python than

Clive Barker. But, on these two occasions, our banter laid the groundwork for these two spine-tingling stories.

"Bearded Vulture" found its rebirth here as a novella after its first life as a short screenplay. Many thanks to Paul Drydyk for reading the story in its early form. Your support gave me the nudge I needed—like diving untethered from a high cliff—to pursue a passion I lost track of back when we were slinging rock and roll around the Midwest.

I'd like to give credit to Scott Smith, author of the classic novel *The Ruins*. That incredible and terrifying book served as a huge inspiration to my story, "Get to the Root of the Problem."

Thanks, also, to Devin Hansrote, a reader of early drafts who kept me grounded during the editing process.

As always, thanks to Jason Then, my editor and friend, without whom none of this happens. Our slasher movie marathons may have been just killing time back in the day, but they weren't for nothing. And those are still some of my fondest memories from those years.

Thanks to the team at Ludovico Treats Publishing. Real horrorshow. But most of all, thanks to anyone who has taken the time to read these stories. I hope they've left you paranoid and checking over your shoulder. Because the only way to live is a little bit frightened all the time.

A.P.B.
Goyang, Korea
October, 2025

About the Author

Anton Brinza was born in 1983 in Milwaukee, Wisconsin. He is the author of the short story collection *The Entire Goat (Entrails Included)*, as well as the forthcoming horror novel *The Coyotes' Cross Prowler*, the first entry in a horror series called *The EORYX Saga*. He has also written a non-horror novel, *Strike, Stay Your Hand*. When not writing, he can generally be found consuming horrors, playing the drums, or crafting homemade hot sauce. He lives with his wife and dog in South Korea.

www.ingramcontent.com/pod-product-compliance
Lightning Source LLC
Chambersburg PA
CBHW032307310726
48973CB00008B/2546